Richard Hyett Warner

Life and Legends of Saint Chad

bishop of Lichfield - 669-672

Richard Hyett Warner

Life and Legends of Saint Chad
bishop of Lichfield - 669-672

ISBN/EAN: 9783337391218

Printed in Europe, USA, Canada, Australia, Japan

Cover: Foto ©Andreas Hilbeck / pixelio.de

More available books at **www.hansebooks.com**

LIFE AND LEGENDS

OF

Saint Chad,

BISHOP OF LICHFIELD, (669—672).

WITH EXTRACTS FROM UN-EDITED MSS.,
AND ILLUSTRATIONS,

BY

REV. R. HYETT WARNER, M.A.

CORPUS CHRISTI COLLEGE, CAMBRIDGE ; CURATE
OF WRYDECROFT, THORNEY.

WISBECH : LEACH & SON ;

LONDON : BELL & DALDY ; CAMBRIDGE : DEIGHTON, BELL & Co.

WISBECH;

LEACH AND SON, PRINTERS,

26, HIGH STREET.

TABLE OF CONTENTS.

LIST OF ILLUSTRATIONS.

ERRATA.

Page 44. I am, unfortunately, unable to recall the exact title of the letter referred to.

Page 60, for "utarur" read "utatur."

for "coryoris" read "corporis."

PREFACE.

AS the life of a Saxon Bishop of the seventh century is hardly a subject which an unpractised pen might be expected spontaneously to choose for a first effort, a few words seem needed to account for the appearance of the present volume.

Saint Chad, though better known as Bishop of Lichfield, was, for some time, abbat of a monastery supposed to have been situated in the modern parish of Lastingham. This parish, though not populous, is very extensive, comprising several scattered hamlets, in one of which, a scheme has been set on foot for the erection of a District Church. By way of assisting the fund, now being raised for this purpose, the writer was induced, by friends interested in the project, to draw up a short LIFE OF SAINT CHAD, the patron saint, so to speak, of the parish. His original design did not extend beyond a small tract for local circulation, but as materials accumulated upon his hands, the modest tract has assumed a more ambitious form, in the little volume now, with much diffidence, submitted to the indulgent reader.

Should the critic ever vouchsafe to notice so small a work, the propriety of a presbyter of the Anglican Communion writing the Life of a Canonized Saint, may, perhaps, be called in question. From an ultramontane point of view, a person canonized by Rome is, so to speak, the exclusive property of the See which enrolled him in the Calendar. Hence, one, who does not acknowledge the authority which declared him to be a saint, may not be thought capable of understanding, much less of pourtraying, those graces, which won for their possessor so glorious a distinction in the Catholic Church. It will, however, be seen, in the following pages, that, while I have endeavoured to do justice to the character of this ancient bishop of our Church, I have only made use of the title of "Saint," given to him by the Bishop of Rome, as a historical designation, which it would have been inconvenient, if not impossible, to suppress.

Read in the light of ecclesiastical history, and modern thought, the education of the Teuton monk at the feet of Celtic doctors, his elevation to the Northumbrian see, founded by the missionaries of Gregory, and his consecration by bishops representing converging lines of Apostolic succession, invest Chad with an exceptional interest; while

A

the deep personal piety, and fervent zeal, he displayed in his two episcopates, shed a beautiful light upon the cradle of the Church he served so well.

The pen of the biographer has been worthily employed in recording the labours of those brave and pious men, who, at the risk of their lives, have carried the Gospel from England to so many heathen lands; but, surely, the pioneers of Christianity, among the people who have given to England herself, a name and renown, deserve no less to be held in grateful remembrance. Of these apostolic men, Saint Chad is allowed, on all hands, to have been one of the most earnest and successful, as he certainly has been one of the most honoured of the Anglo-Saxon bishops.

None the less does the writer feel, that the interest of the present volume will largely depend upon matters not strictly biographical. In the life of a mediæval saint this is inevitable. The prayers and legends, which, to one who receives, without doubt or hesitation, whatever may have have obtained the sanction of the Roman Church, belong to the realm of devotion; for one of a less robust faith, can have, at the most, a deeply human interest, as illustrating the manners and belief of a bygone age.

A word as to the legends themselves. They must by no means be confounded with authentic history, but yet they are most instructive. The monks, like other men, sailed in quest of the ideal, as Saint Brendan sailed in quest of the Fortunate Isles; and if they sought it, after their own fashion, in enchanted forests, or thought to find it in the persons of hero-saints, were they less successful than the crowd of poets and philosophers who are ever returning from the same disappointing voyage?

With respect to the materials made use of in this book, it is hardly needful to say that Venerable Bede is the chief, and almost only, authority, that learned historian deriving his information from the monks of the monastery of which Chad had been abbot. A life of Saint Chad is said to have been written by Daniel, seventh Bishop of Winchester; but, as far as I have been able to ascertain, it is not now extant; otherwise, much additional information would, probably, have been accessible.

Besides the printed sources of information, I have made use of a metrical life of Saint Chad, existing in MS., and attributed to Robert of Gloucester. As this document, in its original form and orthography, would have been hardly intelligible to the general reader, I have gladly availed myself of a version made from a MS. in Corpus Christi College, Cambridge, kindly furnished me by the Rev. W. M. Snell, Fellow of that Society. To the same gentleman I am indebted for a transcript of a mutilated Cottonian MS., of which extracts are given, relating the martyrdom of SS. Wulfade and Rufine, said to have been converted by our saint.

The pleasant task remains, of acknowledging my obligations to other friends at a distance, who have, in various ways, helped me in my little undertaking. Amongst these I must especially not omit to thank the Rev. R. D. Easterby, Vicar of Lastingham, for some written and printed memoranda. bearing upon the subject, which he collected and kindly placed at my disposal; nor must I forget to notice the kindness of W. C. Gresley, Esq., who, at the request of the Rev. Canon Lonsdale, has most courteously examined this life of one, in whom some interest still survives amid the scene of his former labours. Though at the risk of unduly extending this preface, I should be, indeed, ungrateful were I to pass over in silence the many valuable suggestions made in the course of the work by my friend and neighbour the Rev. F. Jackson.

With respect to the illustrations, I can only regret that the circumstances under which the book is published, have not allowed me to do full justice to the drawings generously furnished me by friends. The more fitting it is that I should publicly thank them, for permitting the productions of their pencils to appear in their present humble guise.

From the foregoing remarks it will have been seen that the work is due to external, rather than internal, causes. I can, however, truly say that its preparation has afforded me real pleasure, and that I part from it with regret. In committing it to the press, I shall only be too thankful, if, in spite of the infirmity cleaving to all human efforts, it should be the humble instrument of inducing any one in the ancient kingdoms of Mercia and Northumbria, to emulate the gentle spirit and holy zeal of this ancient prelate, or even if it should advance the work of God but a little, in a hamlet where his voice was heard, twelve hundred years ago, but which is still without its village church !

CHAPTER I.

How beautiful your presence, how benign,
Servants of God ! who not a thought will share
With the vain world ; who outwardly as bare
As winter trees, yield no fallacious sign
That the firm soul is clothed with fruit divine !
Such Priest, when service worthy of his care
Has called him forth to breathe the common air,
Might seem a saintly Image from its shrine
Descended :

WORDSWORTH.

IT was one of the many beautiful conceptions of Greek mythology to place the scroll of History in the hands of the first of the nine sisters of the god of music and poetry. One could almost wish, so that she appeared in Christian guise, that the Muse were still a living personality, rather than a creation of poetic fancy, that she might tell of the divine harmony underlying the discords of the world, and quell with her song the evil spirit which would give up the Universe to the rule of Chance or Fate.

Trusting to no such blind deities, but in the wisdom of the All-loving Father, Religion dries the tears of sorrow, and solves the dark enigmas of History. The ages, which, in the eyes of those who lived in them, were given over

B

to anarchy and chaos, are seen by posterity to have been overshadowed by the darkness which preceded a glorious dawn.

One of the darkest of these epochs was the seventh century of the Christian era. Like the son of an exiled prince, it was ushered into the world amid sorrow and shame. The future of the human race, save to the eye of faith, was shrouded in deepest gloom. The stupendous fabric of civilization and power which kings and consuls, tribunes and emperors, had built up, and which seemed to offer some guarantee for the tranquillity of mankind, had been dismantled and overthrown, but the mystic power which has since overshadowed the world, was even then rising upon its ruins.

In the East the splendid genius of Justinian, though aided by the sword of Belisarius, had striven in vain to recall the kingly spirit which had reared the throne of his predecessors. The provinces which still received their rulers from Constantinople were torn by religious dissensions. The blood of true believers, mingled with that of heretics in shameful disputes concerning the Person of Him, who said, " By this shall all men know that ye are my disciples, if ye have love one to another." The fury of the contending factions was hardly less injurious to the Church than that of the ferocious hordes who flocked round the banner of the Arabian prophet.

But the Spirit of God was moving upon the face of these troubled waters. From the dreary annals of this age one event stands out in noble relief to the sad tale of its sins and sorrows. This was the conversion of the Northern Nations to Christianity, which, though commenced in previous centuries was mainly accomplished in this. No such accessions to Christ's earthly kingdom take place by chance, but in obedience to natural laws, and to God's providential government. Amid the infinite fluctuations of ancient populations, now so difficult to trace, there was a race silently preparing, like a saint in his solitude, to take a noble part in the future history of mankind. When, to the splendid gifts which the Teuton race had received from nature, were added the costlier gifts of grace, a new and glorious career was opened to the people whose savage virtues overthrew the power of Rome and inherited the mantle of her world-wide dominion. Like those curiously wrought vessels found in pagan tombs, and afterwards by a beautiful ritual consecrated to Christian uses, the unknown tribes which followed the standards of the Gothic leaders only awaited admission into the Catholic Church to turn their swords against its foes, and to lay their gifts upon its altars. Whatever may have been the voice crying in this northern wilderness, "Prepare ye the way of the Lord," no nations have gone out to listen to it in like manner since. It has been well observed "that nothing of the

" same kind has happened for more than a thousand years.
" The world is still in large proportion heathen. Christianity
" is indeed still spreading, but mainly by the spread and
" migration of those races whose conversion was completed
" then."*

But it is from that portion of this great family which
made Britain its home, that the following piece of biography will derive its chief interest.   The reception of our
forefathers into the fold of Christ may be regarded as a
very natural, but is certainly the most glorious event in our
history.   To the light, then kindled, England owes her
religion and learning, her literature and fame.   From this
first great stirring of the hearts of the people has flowed
every religious movement, and nearly every political revolution which has since taken place in these islands.   Upon
the foundation, then laid, has been reared the noble fabric
of our civil and religious liberty.   Yet the pen of the
historian seldom lingers upon this noble part of our annals.
It hastens on to describe with dramatic effect the wars and
pageants of later times.   But no tale of mediæval romance,
no record of missionary effort, can surpass in interest the
story of our forefathers' conversion to the true religion of
humanity.   It is full of stirring scenes, dramatic situations,
and deeply touching incidents.   The Gospel of Christ
played then, as it ever will do, upon the noblest and

* Good Words, August, 1869.

tenderest chords of the human heart, and is woven for ever into the fabric of our national life.

Like most of the memorable events of history this great religious movement assumes a deeper interest the more it is read in the light of personal character. What manner of men were those who persuaded our pagan forefathers to forego their hopes of Valhalla, with its golden halls, for the Christian paradise? What was the secret of that eloquence which threw down the temples of Odin and Thor, and raised in their stead in every village of our land its silent witness to the presence of God? By what spell was this race of conquerors itself subdued, and they who came hither to set up earthly kingdoms themselves led captive by the King of Kings and Lord of Lords? The full answer to all this is enshrined in the very bosom of Christianity itself, albeit in the lives of these good men some faint echoes of it may perchance be heard.

A superficial study of the characters of these early pioneers of Christianity amongst us may give rise to a feeling of disappointment. Few of them have found a place in the philosophy, or left their mark, upon the literature of the world. But God hath ever " chosen the weak things of the world to confound the things which are mighty, and things which are not, to bring to nought the things that are." As our Lord chose the humble fishermen and tax-gatherers of Galilee to lay the foundations of His

Church, so this great Church and people are the noblest monument of the labours of those who first preached the Gospel to the Teuton conquerors of Britain.

For what is known of the Apostles of Christianity in Britain, we are mainly indebted to the pen of the Venerable Bede. His history furnishes a complete gallery of ecclesiastical portraits, in some cases, perhaps, not more like the originals, than the figures in the Bayeux tapestry are like the knights who fought, and fell, on the field of Hastings. Yet the intelligent reader of Bede will value the credulity and quaintness pervading his work as illustrating the age in which he lived; the honesty and good nature conspicuous in every page he will welcome as the author's own. With the help of these valuable qualities in the historian, and a little thought, a very good notion may be obtained of the eminent persons whose lives he has recorded. Among them we see newly-converted kings struggling manfully to bring their fierce subjects to the obedience of Christ : others throw off the unwelcome yoke altogether, and vanish into utter darkness and apostacy. Others, too, are seen weary of the weight of royalty, and

> "Leaving human wrongs to right themselves,
> Care but to pass into the silent life."

Loud indeed is the historian in his praises of the holy women whom God raised up, to rebuke by their gentle manners and their holy lives, the fierce and licentious spirit

of their age. What Englishman can read without deep
interest the story of good Queen Bertha, paving the way in
her husband's court by the eloquence of love, for the
preaching of Augustine ? Or of her daughter, Ethelburga
the bride of king Edwin, and the fair herald of the
Gospel in Northumbria ?

Stern, too, were the criticism which would tear away
the veil from the face of Saint Bega, the first of our
English nuns, to disclose the possibly mistaken woman,
fleeing from her father's court to dwell among the fishermen
of Cumberland ; which could hear no echo of the Gospel
in the self-denial which snatched her from the world to
present her as a living sacrifice to the Church ; or which
could see nothing to revere in her friend Saint Hilda,
whose queenly bearing and Christian virtues made her the
fitting guardian, and her monastery the happy home, of
the daughters of kings ; "whom," says the old legend, "all
that knew her called mother, for her singular piety and
grace." With which two saints may be fitly linked in holy
renown, Saint Ebba, sister of king Oswald. Like them,
she laboured long and well among her semi-pagan countrymen ; and the light which now quivers over the northern
waves, from the headland bearing her name, preserves her
memory and is a fitting emblem of her virtues.

But, as might be expected, in a monastic writer, the
mitre and the cowl claim even more attention than the

virgin's veil.   The admiration bestowed by Bede upon some
of the ecclesiastics of his time, is as genuine as it was in
most instances well deserved.   Many of them owe their
fame entirely to his pen.   As these men pass before us, one
by one, in the silent array of history, we wonder at the odd
opinions and actions recorded in their lives; but beneath
their quaint exterior may be discerned those qualities, which,
in every age, have subjugated the minds and wills of other
men.   Saint Patrick the Apostle of the Irish, Saint Colomba,
who evangelized the Scots, Saint Aidan and Saint Cuthbert
of Lindisfarne, were men, who, in any age, or in any walk
of life, would have towered above their fellows, and won a
place in the annals of mankind.

In the foreground of this picture of saints and virgins
and confessors, may be discerned the faint outlines of four
brothers, all accounted righteous men in their generation.
They all served the Church in the sacred office of the
priesthood, and it was fondly noted in the Breviaries
that their number was that of the Evangelists.   All of
the brothers strove, very earnestly, to win the hearts of
their pagan countrymen to the Gospel of Jesus Christ; but
two of them met with such success in their labours,
that their names were enrolled in the Calendars of the
Catholic Church, and they were venerated in after ages
as Saint Chad and Saint Cedd.   Upon this similarity
in their names, Fuller remarks in his quaint way, " A

" brace of brothers, both bishops, both eminent for learning
" and religion, now appeared in the Church, so like in name,
" they are often mistaken in authors one for another. Now
" though it be pleasant for brethren to live together in
" unity yet it is not fit by error they should be jumbled
" together in confusion." Of these two brothers, Saint
Chad became very dear to the hearts of his countrymen,
not only on account of the untiring zeal with which he
sought to promote their eternal interests, but also for the
humble and gentle manner with which he ever enforced
the doctrines he proclaimed, so strongly contrasting with
the lordly mein of many who laboured in the same holy
cause. Chad played an important part in the religious
movements of his time, and, as a popular saint, has found
a place in legend and in song, from which he is even better
known than from his place in the Calendar.

The historian does not record the exact date of his birth,
but it must have taken place early in the seventh century.
Nor does he mention where he was born; and we are left
to infer from several passages in his, and other works that
Chad was an Angle by birth and a native of Northumbria.
Even this has been a matter of dispute. Thomas Demp-
ster, who is described as a learned, but inaccurate writer,
who filled the chair of philology at Pisa, in Italy, in James
the First's time, wrote in Latin an account of Scottish
Saints in a work entitled *Menologium Scotorum* or Scottish

c ·

Menology. Amongst these saints he includes Chad, and states, but without naming his authority, that his bones were carried to Dundraim, and there devoutly interred. The orthodoxy and patriotism of this writer may have induced him to make the most of the fact, that, in Anglo-Saxon times, Northumbria included part of Scotland ; or, he may have been misled by the circumstance that Chad adhered to the Scottish party in the theological controversies of the time. On the other hand the Irish writers did not* suffer it to be forgotten that the *Scoti*, like Colomba, once sailed from the green shores of Ireland. The learned Colgan willing to place a leaf in the saintly crown of Erin, reckons Saint Chad among the pious Irishmen of former days, on the strength, however, of his having spent some years of his youth in Ireland. But there can be no reasonable doubt that the home of Chad was in the land which gave birth to Cuthbert and Bede, to Wilfrid and Cœdmon, and many other lights of the Anglo-Saxon Church.

In prouder, if not happier days, Northumbria extended from the Humber to the Firth of Forth, far beyond the wall which Hadrian had vainly erected as a rampart against the Caledonians. At the royal fortress of Bamborough, overlooking the Northern Sea, its princes maintained a splendid court, and held at bay the ferocious pirates, who were even then becoming the scourge of the eastern coast. More than one of them was invested with the dignity of Bretwalda ;

between them and the Mercian Kings wavered the balance of power in the heptarchy, until the sceptre passed to the descendants of Cerdic.

No part of England has changed more in outward appearance, than this ancient kingdom. Could Saint Chad visit once more this scene of his earthly labours, he might well be amazed at the changes which the lapse of ages has brought about. The mighty forests in which he roamed have given place to cultivated fields; the hamlets, familiar to his childhood, have grown into gigantic towns; beneath the firm earth whereon he trod toils a race that never heard his voice; beyond the weird and murky mass of clouds, lurid with the blaze of countless fires, he would hardly obtain even a transient glimpse of the blue Northumbrian sky of his boyhood, nor in the turbid waters which bear our colliers to the sea would he recognise the clear streams in which he baptized the first-fruits of his ministry.

The population of Northumbria, in his time consisted chiefly of Angles, who, under their renowned leader Ida, had founded this powerful kingdom. They are thought by some to have been more civilized than their Saxon fellow conquerors, in which case Saint Chad shared, and perhaps illustrated, the gentler qualities of his race.

Of his actual birth, beyond the fact that his parents were Angles, we know nothing. His father was probably of not lower rank than that of thegn, and may well have

been one of the converts of Paulinus. A family which furnished the Anglo-Saxon Church with four earnest preachers
could hardly have been reared in a common home. Unlike, in this respect, some other popular saints, no marvellous
stories have been told of the infancy or childhood of Saint
Chad. No myth, or legend, or pious fable, survives to tell
that the future bishop differed, for good or ill, from other
youths of his time. It was not until he had reached man-
hood that the rich treasures of an earnest and devout
character, accumulated in youth, became known to the
Church.

We first meet with Chad as a pupil of Saint Aidan.
This eminent Christian had been sent by the monks of
Iona, in obedience to a welcome summons from Oswald
king of Northumbria, who had lived among them since the
death of his uncle Edwin and the flight of bishop Paulinus.
The pious king remembered with gratitude the good men
who had instructed and consoled him in adversity, and when
God restored him to the throne of his fathers, applied to
them for teachers to instruct his people in the doctrines of
Christianity. In due time Aidan arrived, and was joyfully
and honourably received by the king. A glorious opening
was thus presented to this Apostolic man. The field
which the earnest Paulinus had been compelled reluctantly
to abandon, was now white with the harvest of souls,
waiting to be gathered into the garners of the Church.

The new bishop did not return to York as the seat of his bishopric, but, out of affection to the scene of his former labours, made choice of the little island of Lindisfarne upon the coast of Northumberland. From the similarity of its physical aspect and moral influence, this island has been aptly called the Iona of Northumbria. It is the last place which a modern bishop would choose for the chief city of his diocese, but it harmonized well with the stern spirit of Celtic asceticism. It would indeed have been difficult to find in the dominions of Oswald a drearier spot than the rocky isle on which Saint Aidan lived and prayed. So narrow was his sea-girt home, that the solemn chants of the pious bishop and his companions must have mingled with the roar of the ocean ever beating upon its shores ; the roof of their humble minster must often have been washed by the spray, as the winds rushed wildly over the Northern sea. Twice a day Lindisfarne ceases to be an island, again, twice a day, the returning tide secludes it from the world :

" Dry shod, o'er sands, twice every day
The pilgrims to the shrine find way :
Twice every day the waves efface
Of staves, and sandal'd feet, the trace."

Such was the home of Aidan the Apostle of Northumbria. It has been said to bear "the impress of melancholy and barrenness." Yet on its forsaken shores was kindled a light which illuminated no small part of England with the blessings of Christianity. It has a story, the interest of

which can never fade away. Hither were brought the ashes
of kings. Here many a Saint watched and prayed. Here,
above all, lived the good Saint Cuthbert, and here he
rested till the evil days came, and the Danes drove the
monks from their island-home; and not before they had
wandered with his coffin, many a weary mile, did they find
the Saint a more tranquil and abiding sepulchre :

> " There deep in Durham's gothic shade
> His relics were in secret laid
>   But none may know the place;
> Save of his holiest servants three,
> Deep sworn to solemn secrecy,
>   Who shared that wondrous grace."

But though the fame of Cuthbert eclipsed that of his
illustrious predecessor, it was Aidan who first made Lindisfarne classic ground. A long line of prelates looked back
to him with filial regard, and for ages maintained the
influence of the traditions he transplanted from Iona.

Unlike other island saints, Aidan did not live alone
at Lindisfarne. Soon after his appointment to the
bishopric, he gathered round him twelve promising youths,
to help and succeed him in the ministry, desiring, even in
outward forms, to follow the example of his Divine Master.

It was one of the many good customs of this excellent
bishop to devote the offerings of the rich to the ransom of
young men from captivity, whom he afterwards trained for
the ministry. Chad was one of his pupils, and may possibly
have been thus rescued from a cruel fate to adorn the

Church with his virtues. In any case he was probably one
of this band of disciples, who first received christian instruction from the lips of Saint Aidan. He could not
have sat at the feet of a better Gamaliel; and the
reader will pardon a brief pause in the life of the pupil, to
obtain a passing glimpse of the illustrious preceptor, to whom
he owed so much. The marvellous stories related of him
by Bede, belong to that dim background of pious legend,
without which the life of a Catholic saint would be tame
and incomplete; how he foretold to some mariners a certain
storm which was to befall them at sea; and how they
quelled it with some consecrated oil with which he had
provided them; how the flames which were destroying the
royal city of Bamborough were turned back at his prayers;
and how the post of the church, on which he was leaning
when he died, remained unconsumed by the fire which laid
the fabric in ashes. Happily for his fame the historian has
chronicled matters far more edifying. Above the turmoil
and clamour of that unsettled age, we catch the echo of his
voice, as he preached the gospel to his Northumbrian flock
in his own Celtic tongue, whilst the king stands at his side
to interpret to his people the words of comfort and peace.
Well might the servant of Christ bewail the fatal field
which robbed the Church of so great an ornament, and
himself of so dear a friend. And when, his other royal
friend, king Oswin of Deira, fell beneath the assassin's sword,

no marvel, that, worn out with toil and sorrow, he followed within twelve days his benefactor to the tomb.

But, till death released him from earthly cares, he laboured hard and successfully in his enormous diocese. Chad led no idle life under the eye of Aidan. The bishop required the young men, who studied under him, to devote much of their time to the reading of the Holy Scriptures, and to learning by heart large portions of the Psalter. To these devout and useful studies they doubtless owed much of their future success as missionaries. In the intervals of study, we may imagine these good men coasting along the Northumbrian shore in their convent boat; or at the ebbing of the tide passing over to the adjacent hamlets, two and two, to preach the gospel, and returning to pour the tale of their successes or reverses into the ears of their father in the faith.

How long Chad remained at Lindisfarne we cannot tell, but it was probably at the death of his friend, bishop Aidan, in 651, that he proceeded to Ireland where we next meet with him. His object was to devote himself to the study of the Holy Scriptures, and to "a life of continence and prayer." In coming to Ireland he ascended still higher the stream of Celtic learning, and his after life shows how deeply he imbibed the austere spirit of the Celtic Church. Religion and learning had long flourished in this "virgin isle" to an extent unknown in those countries which had been subdued by Roman arms. Whilst the power of the Cæsars was crumbling into ruins, Ireland was fulfilling the mission ascribed to the Celtic race,* that of supplying the link between Latin and Teutonic civilization. Her chroniclers tell, with just pride, of the illustrious strangers who flocked to her shores, that they might pursue their sacred studies in tranquillity, and sit at the feet of the most renowned sages in Christendom.

Here Chad enjoyed the friendship of more than one holy man, belonging to what is known in history, as the third order of Irish Saints. This order was not so highly esteemed as the two preceding, for, whereas the first order was most holy, the second very holy, this third was only holy; and, whereas the first shone like the Sun, the second like the Moon, the third only reflected the pale light of the Stars. But though these saints were held in less esteem than those who had gone before them, they surpassed them in the austerity of their lives. Their mode of living is well described by, and perhaps suggested the well-known lines:

> "No flocks that roam the valley free
> To slaughter I condemn;
> Taught by the power that pities me,
> I learn to pity them.
> But from the mountain's grassy side
> A guiltless feast I bring;
> A scrip with herbs and fruits supplied,
> And water from the spring."

One of these austere fathers, with whom Chad became

* Ozanam, Etudes Germaniques.

D

acquainted, was the celebrated Egbert, who afterwards was Abbot of Iona, and won over the stubborn sons of Colomba, to the ritual and discipline of Rome. They are said to have studied together at the monastery of Rathmelsigi. This place has been usually identified with Melfont, in the County of Louth, in which case, the history of Chad is connected with one of the chief monastic glories of Ireland. Here, says the learned Dr. O'Connor, the saint was instructed, not only in grammar, rhetoric, metre, geometry, and sacred learning, but, also, in the Irish language; an acquirement of the greatest value to those who were to proclaim to their own countrymen the gospel which they received from the lips of Irish teachers.

As time rolls on, the sad story of Ireland deepens in painful and perplexing interest; but across the centuries of anarchy and misrule through which she has passed, Englishmen may well look back with gratitude to those palmy days, when the doctors of Ireland received our youth to their humble homes, and set before them, without stint or hope of recompense, the treasures of their sacred lore.

CHAPTER II.

" Oh ! hide me in thy temple, arc serene,
  Where safe upon the swell of this rude sea
I might survey the stars, thy towers between,
  And might pray always, not that I would be
Uplifted, or would fain not dwell with thee
On the rough waters, but in soul within
  I sigh for thy pure calm, serene and free ;
I too would prove thy Temple, 'mid the din
Of earthly things unstained by care or sin."

THE CATHEDRAL.

N the edge of the extensive moor which stretches some thirty miles inland from the Yorkshire coast lies the ancient and picturesque village of Lastingham. It is sheltered on the south by a range of hills forming the northern termination of the elevated table land of Ryedale. The sides of these hills clothed to their summits with fern, and crowned with waving pines, form a bold but not unpleasing back-ground to the little landscape in the fore-ground of which the hoary tower of the old parish Church stands out in clear and well-defined relief. Between the village and the moor, wind several small and shallow springs, to whose " perpetual waters," it is said to owe its name and perhaps its existence. One of these streams is spanned by a small stone bridge, over which a

D 2

narrow road leads by a steep ascent to the higher land
above, which, coming to an abrupt termination within a few
hundred yards of the village, affords a beautiful prospect
of the purple moorland beyond.

Almost at the very edge of this projecting platform has
been placed of late years, a plain stone cross surrounded by
a seat inviting the stranger to rest and moralize.   And
surely the eye is not to be envied which can gaze without
delight at the scene here presented to the view, or the
mind to which it suggests no food for serious thought.

Even when the sun is highest in the heavens, the moor
is not without an air of sombre but not unpleasing melancholy, an impression which is rather heightened than
diminished by the distant and sullen-looking shaft of the
Ironworks erected of late years in the vicinity.   But the
approach of night recalls many a tragic story of travellers
perishing of cold upon its inclement bosom, or meeting a
sudden grave in one of the many ravines by which it is
intersected.   History suggests associations of a still more
tragic character.   The moor now so calm and peaceful,
which echoes back no harsher sound than the distant baying
of the sportsman's dog, may once have gleamed with the
camp-fires of the cohorts of Agricola ; the purple heather
and the yellow gorse with which it is so richly clad, once
were dyed with a far sadder hue, when the ruthless Danes,
attracted to Lastingham by the hope of spoil, and their

thirst of blood, destroyed this home of ancient piety and put its defenceless inmates to the sword.

Like many of the villages of our land, Lastingham owes its fame entirely to religion. The Church stands upon the foundation of an old Celtic monastery, and almost within the boundary of the parish may be seen the ruins of the Cistercian priory of Rosedale. The spirit of devotion which once filled the place still hovers round its precincts and invests them with the features of a subtle and suggestive beauty.

Lastingham cannot boast the wild and romantic scenery of earlier monastic sites; though Bede states that the monastery was built amid lofty and distant mountains, there are no hills here to be compared with the granite peaks which frown upon the home of Colomba. The breakers which fill the Cave of Fingal with their hollow murmur, or which beat upon the shores of Lindisfarne are wanting here. But in sight of that wide expanse of moorland, one hardly misses the sea. Not less faithfully than the ocean itself, it reflects the shadow of every passing cloud and records each fleeting change in the heavens above; and though the keenest eye cannot discern the white crests of the distant billows, yet on a calm summer's evening the quick ear can detect the roll of the surge as it washes the strand once trodden by the saintly feet of Hilda.

This secluded spot was for some years the tranquil home

of Chad, from whom it derives its chief interest in ecclesiastical writings. The story of its foundation by his brother
Cedd may be read with interest even now. This prelate
had already preached the gospel successfully in the kingdom
of Mercia, which had been the last of the Saxon states to
embrace Christianity. He was now bishop of the East
Saxons, amongst whom he had recovered much of the
ground which had been lost in the time of bishop Mellitus,
when nearly all the people fell away from the faith. Amid
the cares of this enormous diocese it was a welcome
relief to the good bishop sometimes to visit his old friends
in the North, especially his brother Celin who was living
in the household of Ethelwald, king of Deira, son of the
famous Oswald, to whom and his family he was wont to
administer the word and the sacraments of the faith. This
prince, finding Cedd to be a holy and wise man and of a
good disposition, desired him to accept some land to build
a monastery, to which he himself might frequently resort,
to offer his prayers to the Lord, and hear the word and be
buried in it when he died. " The bishop complying with the
king's desires," continues Bede, "chose himself a place to
build a monastery among lofty and distant mountains, which
looked more like lurking-places for robbers and retreats for
wild beasts, than habitations for men, to the end that according to the prophecy of Isaiah ' In the habitations where
before dragons dwelt might spring up grass with reeds and
rushes,' that is, that the fruits of good works should there

spring up, where before beasts were wont to dwell, or men
to live after the manner of beasts."

But before a beam of the sacred building could be hewn,
or even a sod turned for its foundation, many a holy prayer
must be offered up, many a solemn litany chanted. Wherefore proceeds our author, "the man of God, desiring first to
cleanse the place which he had received for the monastery
from the pollution of former crimes, by prayer and fasting,
that it might become acceptable to our Lord, and so to lay
the foundations of the monastery, requested of the king that
he would give him leave to reside there all the approaching
time of Lent, to pray. During which days except on the
Sunday, he fasted till the evening, according to custom, and
then took no other sustenance than a very little bread, one
hen's egg, and a little milk mixed with water. This he
said was the custom of those from whom he had learned
the rule of regular discipline ; first to consecrate to our Lord
by prayers and fastings, the places which they had newly
received for building a monastery, or a Church. When
there were ten days of Lent still remaining, there came one
to call him to the king ; and he, that the religious work
might not be intermitted on account of the king's affairs
entreated his priest Cynebil, who was also his own brother,
to complete that which was so piously begun. Cynebil
readily complied, and when the time of fasting and prayer
was over, he there built the monastery now called Læst-

ingaen and established therein religious customs according to the rites of Lindisfarne where they had been educated."

The monastery which Cedd and Cinebil had been thus instrumental in building was to be their own *Lasting-home* ; for so some explain the name of Lastingham.

Bishop Cedd was present at the celebrated synod held at Whitby in the year 664 for the purpose of determining the Easter controversy, on which occasion he acted as interpreter between the Irish and Saxon prelates. It was in this year he came once more to Lastingham, but it was to die. A deadly pestilence was devastating the west of Europe, to which many persons of all ranks of society had already fallen victims. So grievous was the scourge that crowds of people flocked to the sea-side and threw themselves hand in hand from the cliffs, choosing rather to perish by a speedy death beneath the waves than by the lingering torments of the pestilence. In this frightful visitation perished Cedd and his brother Cinebil and were buried at Lastingham. An affecting story is told in connection with Cedd's death, which though not strictly belonging to the course of our narrative, may not be altogether unwelcome to the reader. "When the brethren who were in his monastery of the East Saxons heard that the bishop was dead in the province of the Northumbrians, about thirty men of that monastery came thither, being desirous either to live near the body of their father, if it should please God, or to die there and be buried." Their pious wishes were soon granted. " Being lovingly received by their brethren at Lastingham, all but one perished of the pestilence" and were buried beneath the same green sod which covered their father and their friend. " How is it possible" asks Montelembert, who relates this story, " not to love those rough Saxons, scarce converted, but moved in the cloister by that passionate self-devotion, by that necessity of giving life for the beloved, which in the midst of their natural fierceness continued the distinctive feature of the Anglo Saxon race?"

With his dying breath the bishop committed the care of the sorrowing community to his brother Chad whom we left in Ireland. The circumstances under which he thus became the second Abbot of Lastingham were very depressing, but there was much to encourage an earnest and devout mind to persevere in the work of Christian usefulness. The little brotherhood gathered together at Lastingham was already doing its part towards dispelling the heathen darkness by which it was surrounded. The convent-church in which they prayed was at first built of wood, probably not unlike in appearance the Church still standing at Greenstead, the last of its humble race. The monks' houses would be of the same simple character, for the monks of the Celtic

E

Church in no way resembled the lordly churchmen of later times. More than one eminent ecclesiastic of the age was indebted to Lastingham for Christian instruction. It was from the lips of Chad that Trumbert acquired much of that sacred learning he afterwards imparted to the Venerable Bede, whose grateful pen has rescued the names of both from oblivion.

Sometimes, too, one from the busy world far beyond the Moors would find his way to this sequestered home, where he thought to end his days in peace, far away from the turmoil of those unquiet times. One day a stranger of courteous mein, but clad in humble garb, and bearing upon his shoulder an axe and mattock, presented himself at the gate of the little Minster praying to be received into the company of the holy brethren. This was Ovin, lately steward of the famous and eccentric Queen, Ethelreda. Following the example of his royal mistress, he had turned his back upon a world he could no longer enjoy, and in this humble guise had sought out the home of Chad. Tradition relates that as he pursued his long and toilsome journey from the Fens which surrounded the abbey of Ethelreda, into Yorkshire, the pilgrim erected crosses by the road-side to guide any heavy laden souls who might hereafter seek the same blessed haven of rest. Saint Chad took the devout stranger at his word, asking him no unwelcome questions concerning his worldly gear, and after the hospitable fashion of those simple times gave him a hearty welcome to their humble home and frugal fare. And while the brethren were engaged in preaching the gospel in the adjacent hamlets, or in devout studies at home, he laboured hard with his hands, ministering with all humility to their necessities. We shall meet with this saint again in the course of this history; but it may be interesting to note here that there is preserved in Ely Cathedral a very ancient cross, supposed to have been either erected by Ovin in his life time, or in his honour, after his death, and bearing this inscription :

LVCEM TVAM OVINO

DA. DEVS. ET. REQVIEM

AMEN.

Thus rendered by Doctor Bentham "Grant O God to Ovin Thy light and rest. Amen."

Many a Christian soul has breathed the prayer sculptured upon that ancient cross. Many have sought an answer to it in the "cloistered cell." Thousands, who think scorn of the monks of other days, are still groping for the light, and are no nearer to rest. Only in the newer life shall men dwell in the pure light of God, and exchange the turmoil of earth for the unruffled tranquility of heaven.

To return to our Saint. By the side of these lonely Yorkshire Moors, Chad led for a while a tranquil but laborious life.

One is tempted to paint in more glowing colours than the reality would warrant the life of holy usefulness pursued at such a place as Lastingham, and to forget that it must have had its darker aspect as well. It is, at least, pleasant to picture the shaven missionaries journeying from village to village and preaching the gospel, often for the first time, to those Angles of whom Pope Gregory had said they would have been angels if only they had been Christians; or, by the pale light gleaming across the moor from their sequestered minster, to follow their pens as, with some precious relic of early christianity before them, they transcribe and adorn with many a quaint device and many a holy symbol those superb volumes of Holy Writ, which, long after the fingers that traced them had mouldered in the dust, conveyed the Water of Life to many a weary soul; but, over the inner life of these men, their wrestling with the evil within and around them, their fastings and watchings, their vigils and prayers, their spiritual triumphs, and we must needs add their spiritual delusions, Biography reverently draws the veil.

It has been mentioned that Lastingham was at first a Celtic monastery, though like many others in the north of England, it afterwards embraced the rule of Saint Benedict. The monastic system founded by, or at least reformed by Colomba has often been unfavourably compared with that instituted by Saint Benedict. If the value of such systems be measured by the time during which they lasted, or by the number of distinguished names they have given to the world, then the palm must doubtless be awarded to the milder rule of the monk of Monte Casino. The Benedictines need no modern pen to do justice to their merits. History bears ample witness to their influence on civilization. The libraries of Europe are stored with the treasures which they rescued from antiquity and with the monuments of their own piety and learning. The still higher merit of raising the tone of religion in their age may freely be accorded to the earlier disciples of the great monastic lawgiver. Yet if all monastic institutions be regarded as more or less violating the laws of nature; or, at best, but as a return to a discipline suited only to the childhood of civilization, and to exceptional phases of society, then, perhaps, that system is to be preferred which made the shortest but keenest struggle against the paganism which surrounded it, and having accomplished its mission, perished like a conquering general in the arms of victory. Whether this be a just estimate of the two forms of monasticism or not, there is no doubt that the Celtic monasteries did much for the cause of religion in these islands. They would at least appear to have escaped much of the corruption, which in a later age sealed the doom of their rivals.

Chad was not long to enjoy the peace and retirement of his secluded cell. The Synod at Whitby which had been

called for the ostensible purpose of settling the Easter controversy had ended in a great victory for Rome. The traditions of Iona were condemned and the Church founded by
Saint Aidan bowed down before the chair of Saint Peter.
Wilfrid, to whose eloquence and ambition the result was
mainly due, soon reaped his reward. The Atheling Alchfrid
who governed the kingdom of Deira subject to his father
Oswy had been one of Wilfrid's pupils. The young prince
earnestly adopted the views of his preceptor, and like him
had been dazzled with the splendour of Roman authority.
He had already bestowed upon Wilfrid many substantial
marks of his princely favour, and at the breaking up of the
Synod, apparently with his father's consent, committed to
him the spiritual oversight of his kingdom.

With offensive bigotry, Wilfrid refused to be consecrated
by his ecclesiastical superior the Archbishop of Canterbury,
or by any of the English or British prelates, on the ground
that he was not satisfied with the position in which they
stood to the Holy See. He therefore proceeded to France
and was consecrated by his friend Agilbert who had shared
with him the triumph at Whitby, and had recently been
appointed to the Archbishopric of Paris. His biographers
tell with pride of the eleven bishops who assisted at the
ceremony, and carried the new bishop upon their shoulders
in a golden chair, which none of lower than bishops degree
might presume to touch. How little of apostolic simplicity
was preserved in this imposing ceremonial!

Anxious to increase his stores of learning, or perhaps,
allured by the fascinations of foreign travel, the new prelate
seemed to prefer the banks of the Seine to those of the
Ouse. But whilst he thus unaccountably deferred his return,
the mitre itself was slipping from his grasp. The king
began to chafe with barbarian impatience at the unexpected
delay, and regretted the hasty consent he had given to the
views of his son. The thegns who surrounded his throne,
ill-brooked the ambition which would reduce their king to a
vassal of Rome. The chorus of discontent was swollen by
the voices of those who still believed that the sanction of an
Apostle might be claimed for the usages of their Church.
At length the patience of Oswy was exhausted altogether.
No Wilfrid appeared, and he therefore resolved to provide
the deserted flock with a shepherd. His eyes naturally
turned to what in modern politics would be called the Party
of the Opposition. The Abbot of Lastingham was already
favourably known for his piety and zeal. His brothers
Cedd and Celin had enjoyed the confidence and respect of
the Northumbrian and Mercian Courts. To him therefore the vacant bishopric was offered. Chad's conduct in
accepting the mitre under these circumstances was severely
censured by his Roman contemporaries. "He took possession of another man's bishopric after the manner of a
robber," wrote one; "he had snatched the bride from her
living husband," sang another. The king as naturally came in

for his share of ecclesiastical wrath. He had been deceived, it was said, by persons envious of the decision at Whitby; nay, he was instigated by the Evil One in the appointment of Chad. Modern writers express similar views. Montelembert though describing Chad as "an innocent usurper" and a "holy intruder," attributes to him "a strange forgetfulness of duty" in thus yielding to the wishes of the king. Even the learned writer of the "*Lives of the Archbishops*" vouchsafes him no higher praise than that "he was a good man, though a fanatic."

The account of Chad's appointment to York is derived entirely from writers devoted to Rome. But even from their partial testimony it is not difficult to frame a vindication of the part which he took in the matter. In common with many of his countrymen he naturally regarded the appointment of Wilfrid as a trophy of the victory which had subverted the independence of his Church. With whom, too, had the new bishop "left those few sheep in the wilderness" whilst he basked in the sunshine of splendour and flattery abroad? And when the instincts of patriotism and the necessities of a neglected diocese were supported by the urgent representations of his sovereign, the humble-minded Abbot reluctantly accepted the crozier his rival appeared to despise.

Whether Wilfrid's prolonged absence abroad justified the step taken by the Northumbrian king may be open to doubt,

but it certainly withdrew from his Court that personal influence to which its recent policy had been due, and furnished
the enemies of the absent prelate with a pretext, if not a
motive, for their conduct. In any case, though the course
pursued by Saint Chad has been condemned as uncanonical,
the purity of his motives has never been assailed.

By the desire of Oswy, Chad left Lastingham for Canterbury to be consecrated by the metropolitan, taking with
him, as his companion in travel, one of his monks named
Eadhed. We may well imagine with what deep and
reverent interest the travellers approached the city, which,
even in their time, had become venerable. There rose the
little church of Saint Martin in which good Queen Bertha
and her husband Ethelbert had knelt and prayed. They
would see too, what must, then, have appeared a stately pile
and which grew in later times into the majestic Cathedral
of Saint Peter; where had been heard the voices of Augustine and Honorius, and where they slept when their work on
earth was done.

Disappointment awaited the travellers on reaching the
city. The pestilence, already so frequently mentioned in
these pages, had carried off the primate Deusdedit, to the
great grief of the English people, for he was the first Saxon
priest that had sat in the chair of Augustine. At his death
the kings of Northumbria and Kent had joined in nomina-
ting a successor, whom they sent to Rome to receive the

F

imposition of hands from the Pope himself. But the plague which had raged in England was not less fatal at Rome, and the English Primate sleeps beneath the shadow of the Eternal City.

The news of Wighard's death would not appear to have reached Canterbury when Chad arrived; or, if it had, no successor to the deceased primate had been appointed. From Canterbury, therefore, Chad and his companion turned their steps to Winchester. Under the Roman name of Venta, this place had become one of the most important stations in the island, and, as the capital of the West Saxons, had been chosen as the seat of a bishopric. Birinus, who had been sent by Pope Honorius to preach the gospel to the tribes lying beyond the territories of the Saxons, finding the West Saxons not more enlightened than their British neighbours, took up his abode amongst them and became their first bishop.

At the time of Chad's visit to Winchester, the see was occupied by the celebrated Wini, whom History afterwards branded with the guilt of being the first to pollute the Saxon Church with the sin of simony. On the death of the Primate Deusdedit, he was held by the extreme romanizing party in the Church to be the only bishop in England canonically ordained, by which they meant ordained by bishops in direct communion with the Roman see. It availed naught with these fanatical zealots that the British Prelates who met beneath the shade of Augustine's oak, though urged to submit to Rome, were not required even by that haughty missionary to prove their apostolic descent. Their episcopal character and authority had been virtually acknowledged by Pope Gregory in the letter in which he placed them under the jurisdiction of Augustine as their metropolitan. The presence of British bishops at Nicæa, and at Arles, if not at Ariminum, was alone sufficient to vindicate their Church from the charge of heresy or schism. But for the unhappy accident of Augustine not rising to receive his British colleagues the Prelates of Menevia and Canterbury might have founded, some generations earlier, the Church in which conquered and conquerors were trained to be brothers in Christ.

The successors of these bishops, holding fast as they did to the traditions of their fathers, incurred no guilt of schism save what had been fastened upon them by the servile adherents of Rome, and the student of ecclesiastical history has but little doubt that their orders were as valid as those of any bishops in Christendom.

The consecration of Chad by Bishop Wini possesses, on several grounds, more than a mere biographical interest, and strikingly illustrates the different views taken of the position of the British Church. The ceremony itself took place in the magnificent Church, still fresh from the mason's chisel, which had been commenced by the West Saxon

King, Kinegils, and completed by his successor, Kenwalch. Tradition assigned to the spot a still earlier fabric, said to have been erected by King Lucius, after his conversion, as the first-fruits of his gratitude and zeal.

Wini, unlike Wilfrid, did not regard the British Bishops as in schism, for he invited two of them to assist at the consecration of Chad, and the three together laid their hands upon the head of the Northumbrian Prelate.* Years were to pass away before a National Church was to arise from the fusion of these rival communions, but its dim outline had already shaped itself to the minds of thoughtful men, when Briton and Saxon, together, bestowed the episcopal benediction upon a disciple of Saint Aidan. The two lines of ecclesiastical descent, represented by Wini and his coadjutors, thus met in the consecration of Chad, whose priests and deacons might deduce, with pardonable satisfaction, the origin of their Christianity alike from East and West.

A consecration performed by Bishops of different or rival Churches would, in our time, be regarded as an event highly interesting and auspicious. But it was not so in the seventh century. Rome was already beginning to carry matters with a high hand, and the tendency was towards a

---

* "The terms upon which the Church of Wessex stood respectively to those of Cornwall and of Wales in the time of Aldhelm (Epist. ad Gerunt. A.D. 705) seem to determine these bishops to have been Cornish." Haddan and Stubbs, Ed. of Wilkins' Concilia, Vol. I. p. 124.

Consecration of Chad at Winchester.

suppression of the independence of national Churches by the weight of Roman authority. In the present instance the orthodoxy of Wini, as will be seen later, availed nothing against the alleged schism of his coadjutors.

In the meantime, wholly unconscious of any defect in his consecration, Chad returned to the North to take charge of his widely scattered flock. In the Breviaries there is an antiphon implying that he was Archbishop of York :—

Quem cum bitae sanctitas
Ut lur se monstrabit
Eboraci cibitas
Archipresulabit.

In a metrical life of the Saint, attributed to Robert of Gloucester, he is also invested with the metropolitan dignity :—

The King Oswy was then King of Northumberland,
In St. Chadde the good man each goodness he found,
Archbishop of York he chose him to be there,
And sent him to Canterbury that he consecrated were.

Chad however was not Archbishop of York. Paulinus had enjoyed that dignity, but, at his flight into Kent, it had fallen into abeyance, and it was not until the time of Bishop Egbert, that York received once more the treacherous gift of the Roman pallium. But, though no suffragans acknowledged Chad as their superior, he had ample scope for the most abundant energy. The population he had to deal

with was indeed small compared with that of the modern
province. If every person in the diocese had been baptized,
the population would probably not have equalled that of
the single town of Leeds. But, though the subjects of
King Oswy were few, they were scattered over an extensive
territory. The inhabitants of the towns lying on the great
military roads bequeathed by the Romans to their successors, and on the numerous branch roads, were, doubtless,
easy of access, but it must have been very difficult
to obtain a thorough knowledge of the remoter districts.
More than thirty years had now passed away since
the British prince, Cadwalla, had dyed his sword in the
blood of King Edwin, and though the monks of Lindisfarne had not been idle in the interval, the new
Bishop had almost to recommence the work of evangelizing
Northumbria. His difficulties were not lessened by the
embarrassing condition of affairs which had led to his
appointment. He could not forget that another had been
appointed to his bishopric, and the shadow of the absent
Wilfrid must sometimes have been thrown across his
already troubled path.

But with all these difficulties Chad grappled with the
energy of one of lofty purpose and consecrated will. The
ascetic habits in which he had been trained at Lindisfarne
and in Ireland, though savouring of superstitition, had
taught him to disdain hardships and privations, and thus,

eminently qualified him to labour in a sphere wherein much must be endured, if but a little was to be achieved.

How many clergy acknowledged him as their head, and lightened his toil, we have no means of knowing, but there can be no doubt that if the harvest was plenteous the labourers were but few.

Bede informs us, in the quaint language of the time, that the new Bishop began immediately to devote himself to ecclesiastical truth and to chastity; to apply himself to humility, continence and study; to travel about, not on horseback, but after the manner of the Apostles, on foot; preaching the Gospel in towns, in the open country, in cottages, villages, and castles, for he was one of the disciples of Saint Aidan, and endeavoured to instruct his people by the same actions and behaviour, according to his and his brother Cedd's example.

His consecration and subsequent labours are even more curiously described in the metrical life already quoted:—

Then wended he towards the Marsh to the Bishop Wyne,
Who was then Bishop of the Marsh, to bring this to a fine,
So that, by the Bishop Wyne, he was consecrated then,
He returned to York when this deed was done.
He endeavoured earnestly, night and day, when he had thither come,
To guard well holy Church, and to uphold Christendom.
He went into all his bishopric and preacht full fast,
Much of that folk, through his word, to God their hearts cast,
All afoot he travelled about, nor kept he any state,

Rich man though he was made, he reckoned there of little.
The Archbishop of York had not him used to go
To preach about on his feet nor another none the mo,
They ride upon their palfreys, lest they should spurn their toe,
But riches and worldly state doth to holy Church moe.

Chad's humility in traversing his vast diocese on foot, rather than on horseback, afterwards attracted the notice of Archbishop Theodore, who endeavoured to dissuade him from such needless austerity. Being unable to prevail upon him to omit the pious labour he loved so well, on one occasion the primate induced him to undergo what, to a person unused to the saddle, was probably a still greater austerity ; and by way of silencing all opposition, with his own archiepiscopal hands, lifted the reluctant Bishop on to a steed and dispatched him swiftly on his journey, for he thought so holy a man ought not to walk, and therefore obliged him to ride wherever he had need to go. In a homily, drawn up for use on Saint Chad's day, the saint is described as travelling in a wain, the uncomfortable character of which kind of conveyance, gave it but little advantage over pedestrian exercise.

Beyond this general account of his labours, but few authentic particulars have been preserved, from which to form any vivid notion of the life and character of the man himself. Enough however has been recorded to raise the simple Abbot of Lastingham to the dignity of a Missionary,

Ap. Theodore compels Chad to ride.

almost to grace him with the zeal and devotion of an
Apostle.   When we realize the holy and arduous work of
leavening the North of England with the teaching of Christianity which Chad all but commenced, and which is yet so
far from ended, he drops the garb of the semi-mythical
saint, in which he is commonly regarded ; he steps down
from his place in the Calendar, and mingling with living
men, is straightway invested with a deeply human interest.
He is in the thickest of the deadly affray, ever raging against
the powers of darkness and evil.   He bears aloft the torch
of gospel truth, received from his predecessors, and transmits
it, still beaming, to the age which followed him.   Across the
gulf of time which separates that generation from ours, we
listen to this zealous preacher of the gospel, as he delivers
to his countrymen, assembled in some rustic temple, or in
the rush-strewn hall of some village thegn, the message of
the Eternal to the hearts of men.   We follow him from
hamlet to hamlet, across wild moorlands and through
primeval forests, or along desolate cliffs, the wild haunts
of fishermen and wreckers.   We mingle with the crowd
which gathers round him as he plants his cross in some
northern village ; we hear him tell, in that beautiful, old-
world tongue, which still gives to our modern speech its
greatest charm, the sweet·story of the cross, of its never
failing freshness, of its perpetual symbolism, stirring within
those rugged, but not wholly corrupted hearts, the pulse of

G

a new and heaven-born life, as he unfolds to them the love
of God to man dimly shadowed forth in their own sacred
songs of Balder, but only fully revealed to men in Christ
Jesus our Lord. And as one, who, finding himself, unawares,
on the skirts of a crowd gathered round some earnest
preacher of the gospel, stands for a while in unconscious
homage, to listen to his words, so a self-indulgent age, like
this, may well spare a few moments, from business and
pleasure, to ponder upon the life and labours of this almost
forgotten saint, by the foolishness of whose preaching so
many souls found their way to Christ and peace.

CHAPTER III.

All worship is prerogative, and a flower
Of his rich crown, from whom lies no appeal
    At the last hour :
Therefore we dare not from his garland steal
To make a posy for inferior power.

Although, then, others court you, if ye know
What's done on earth, we shall not fare the worse
    Who do not so ;
Since we are ever ready to disburse,
If any one our Master's hand can show.
                            GEORGE HERBERT.

HE circumstances under which Saint Chad had
been appointed to the northern bishopric, made
the episcopal chair anything but a bed of roses.
Soon after his consecration to the see, Wilfrid, after many
adventures, returned from France to find his throne occupied
by another. It was a very embarassing position for both
prelates. The difficulties of the Church were hardly less
than those which beset the State. King Alchfrid had
nominated Wilfrid, and his father had appointed Chad ; and
the return of the former, to claim his diocese, was an event
by no means calculated to throw oil upon the troubled
waters of Northumbrian politics. Wilfrid, whether from a
feeling that a very natural course had been pursued in his
absence, or from a commendable unwillingness to press his

own claim to the see, wisely forebore to disturb the peace of the diocese, and quietly withdrew to his monastery of Ripon, which the munificence of his royal friend had enabled him to found. For a while, Chad was left in undisturbed possession of the see, which, notwithstanding the doubtful character of his appointment, he is universally admitted to have administered with signal ability and success. Wilfrid was not less usefully employed in the see of Canterbury, the affairs of which he directed until the arrival of the primate from Rome.

But though Chad and Wilfrid are the two most prominent characters in connection with these transactions, a far wider issue than any personal question was involved. The two prelates were but the representatives and exponents of principles, which must, sooner or later, have come into collision.

When the bishops of Rome began to covet the throne of the Cæsars, and to aspire to universal dominion over the Christian Church, their unholy pretensions were speedily confronted by Churches of not less antiquity than their own, and of equally apostolic origin. By slow, but certain, steps, the independence of these Churches crumbled away before the insidious attacks of Rome. These spiritual conquests have been well compared * to the victories, gained by republican and imperial Rome, over those unhappy nations

* Letter of Dr. Wordsworth.

whom the sculptor has pourtrayed winding in sorrowful array round the column crowned with the image of the fortunate master of the Roman world.

The most formidable opponent of Papal authority was the Celtic Church, including within its pale Ireland, a large portion of Scotland, and the northern shires of England. The learning of its prelates, the unrivalled beauty of the manuscripts produced in its monasteries, the traditions of its martyrs and saints and confessors, and, above all, the zeal and success of its missionaries, gave to this Church a strength and vitality against which Rome strove for long in vain. Long after the other Churches of the West had bowed their necks to her yoke, the Celtic Church alone, like another Mordecai, refused to do homage to the Roman Haman. The features of the struggle, which has been waged ever since, between the principle which would subjugate the Church to a visible head, and the other principle which requires loyalty to her Invisible Head, as the true bond of union, are clearly discernible in the transactions in which Chad bore a part. By his appointment the gauntlet had been thrown down to Rome.

Wilfrid's return, as we have seen, made no immediate alteration in the position of affairs, and the character of saint or politician will be given to him less upon his own merits, than upon the bias of the reader. But if any wrong had been done him, in the elevation of Chad to York, it was soon to be set right. The new Archbishop of Canterbury was on his way to England. The kings of Northumbria and Kent had unwittingly played into the hands of Rome, in soliciting from Pope Vitalian the appointment of a Metropolitan in place of the deceased Wighard.

The Pope's choice fell upon the celebrated Theodore of Tarsus. Nurtured in the bosom of the Eastern Church, and stored with the learning of the West, he seemed eminently qualified, by his character and antecedents, to occupy the difficult and exalted position to which he was called. All classes of society were anxious for a settlement of ecclesiastical affairs, and gave a hearty welcome to this "citizen of no mean city."

The new primate at once applied himself to remedy various abuses which had sprung up in the Saxon Church, and to reduce both Saxon and Celtic Churches into one communion, subject to the see of Rome.

One of the first to feel the weight of his crozier was Chad, whose pious and indefatigable labours in the north were now to come to an end. His position as Bishop of York might have been plausibly challenged on the ground that he had been intruded into another bishop's diocese. But the primate, willing, probably, to avoid needless disputes with the Northumbrian king, chose rather to condemn Chad's appointment, on the ground that his consecration had been uncanonical, in consequence of the presence of the two British bishops. This was a most unwarrantable stretch of authority. No canons had been violated in the consecration of Chad, unless all the British bishops were to be regarded as no bishops at all. It was one thing for the primate to lay down a rule for his future guidance, but a very different matter to apply such a rule retrospectively.

But it was plainly Theodore's intention to rule the Church of England as the Pope's representative. Had Chad's consecration been without a flaw in his eyes, there can be little doubt, that he would have required him to vacate a see to which he had been appointed in defiance of Rome. But Oswy could not confer the pallium, and the absence of this much coveted symbol left Chad within the jurisdiction, if not, at the mercy, of the high-handed metropolitan.

To overbearing authority, Chad opposed the most truly Christian humility. To be thus called upon to resign a bishopric to which he believed himself rightfully appointed, and to divest himself of a rank in the Church, to which, in the judgment of all but Theodore, he had been canonically raised, would have been a great trial to the saintliest and meekest of men. Chad met it nobly. To the reproaches of the Archbishop he replied in the true spirit of the Christian; "If you are persuaded that I have not duly received episcopal ordination, I willingly resign the office, for I never thought myself worthy of it, but, though unworthy, in obedience to authority submitted to undertake it."

Struck with the spectacle of such truly Christian meekness, Theodore hastened to assure the good bishop that,
though his consecration had been uncanonical, and he must
therefore resign the see, yet he would by no means deprive
him of his episcopal rank, but would complete his consecration after the canonical manner.   There has been some
difference of opinion as to what ecclesiastical steps Chad
was required to go through, at this time.   But it is a needless
enquiry.   His real offence was not in the manner, but in the
fact of his appointment, for which there was no remedy but
his deposition.

The protestant reader may possibly think that Chad
should have made a firmer stand against papal encroach-
ments and the arbitrary authority of the Primate.   But
bishops are not prophets.   No man at that time could have
foreseen the debasing tyranny and corruption under which
the Western Churches were to groan for ages.   It would
have needed a keen eye to pierce the secret recesses of the
Vatican, where the papal Vulcan was forging his chains to
bind the Christian Prometheus to his rock.   Moreover the
ecclesiastical polity of England had yet to be settled ; principles had to be tried and experience gained.   The confident
assertions of Theodore would naturally create doubts in the
mind of Chad, and unless he was fully persuaded of the
justice of his cause, the meeker, was probably, also, the wiser
course.

Although the first episcopate of Chad was brief, it is on many accounts deeply interesting. As the first Saxon bishop of York, and the successor, after a long interval, of the Italian Paulinus, he stands upon the threshold of a new era in the history of British Christianity.

The church, whose origin tradition fondly traced to the disciple who embalmed our Lord, which had been enriched by the blood of Saint Alban, and defended by king Arthur's sword, had waxed feeble and corrupt beneath the shield of the empire, and was fast vanishing like the Holy Grail itself into the myth of a golden age. The other branch of the Celtic church had borne noble fruit at Lindisfarne, and to the successful zeal of its missionaries was due the conversion of the greater part of the territory conquered by the Angles and Saxons.

But as the new conquerors embraced Christianity they introduced a fresh ecclesiastical element into the country. Bound by no ties of gratitude to the Church whose priests they had slain, and whose altars they had overthrown, they wavered for a while in their allegiance between Iona and Rome. But the return of Wilfrid to England, laden with the traditions, and infected with the spirit of Rome, had a marked influence upon the course of our ecclesiastical history. He was the first of a long line of pilgrims, who have since been led by piety or curiosity to visit the city of the Cæsars. From that time the fatal spells of the

II

Papacy began to be thrown around the infant churches.
Gratitude for spiritual benefits already received, admiration
of the superior civilization of Rome, and the desire to be
received within the community of nations of which she was
the head, eventually brought our forefathers to the chair of
Saint Peter, though their spirit was never wholly subdued
nor their ecclesiastical independence altogether lost.

The nomination of Wilfrid and afterwards of Saint Chad
to the see of York, founded by Gregory, rather than to that
of Lindisfarne, founded by Aidan, plainly shewed the
path upon which the Church had entered.

Saint Chad's elevation to the see occurred at the very
time, when the English church, if the designation may be
anticipated, was trembling in the balance of its future destiny.
Though brought up at the feet of Saint Aidan and versed
in all the lore of the Celtic church, he could not resist
what many will condemn as Roman influence and not a
few have praised as a catholic instinct.   This apparent
want of fidelity to the principles in which he had been
educated may deprive him of the sympathy of many who
admire his virtues, but it should not be forgotten that he
was surrounded by the mental and moral problems belonging
to a period of change and transition.   A man of sterner
character might have protracted, but could not alter the
result of, the struggle.   His lot was cast at the junction of
two impetuous streams, and no one can blame him that
he was carried away by their united and foaming torrent.

But though Chad accepted the Roman ritual and doctrine, as then ascertained, he was no ultramontane. He never became a Romanist as opposed to a Catholic. The ungodly pretentions of the so-called Holy See had not yet shivered to atoms the glorious unity of the Church, or disturbed the balance of her spiritual power.

The real value of Saint Chad's episcopate was in the zeal and success with which he instructed his heathen countrymen in the doctrines of the Christian· faith and morals, and in the beautiful commentary which a blameless life afforded to his lofty teaching. The voices of his contemporaries join in the chorus of his praise even when he was raised to the throne of Wilfrid.* " Admirabilem doctorem de Hibernia" wrote one of his rival's biographers. In more poetic guise, sang another writer† of the same saint's life :

"Moribus acclinem, doctrinæ robore fortem."

Bede, whose information was derived from the monks of Lastingham, describes him as " a holy man, of modest beha-" viour, sufficiently well read in the scriptures and diligently " practising those things which he had learned therein." Subsequent writers confirmed the opinions of their predecessors, and described Saint Chad, in language ill-suited to many of the mitred statesmen who followed him, as having ruled his diocese " sublimely."

* Eddius' Life of Wilfrid.
† Fridegod's Life of Wilfrid in Mabillon's Acts of the Benedictines.

On one occasion only we seem to have a glimpse of
Saint Chad officiating in the cathedral church of York, but
the vision melts away at the first touch of criticism. We learn
from an old chronicle * how that Saint Cuthbert, after many
refusals, at length yielded to the earnest entreaties of king
Egfrid and his subjects and became their bishop ; how
amid many tears he quitted his rock-hewn cell in the Island
of Farne, and was consecrated at York, by Archbishop
Theodore and six bishops, amongst whom were Chad,
bishop of Lichfield, and Cedd, bishop of the East Saxons.
It would be pleasant to think of the history of two of the
most illustrious saints in the Calendar being thus connected,
and to believe that their labours were lightened by mutual
counsel and help; but at the time of Cuthbert's consecration
to the bishopric of Hexham, Chad had long entered upon
his rest.

The same chronicle records that various lands were
granted for the endowment of the bishopric, and recites a
charter conveying the town of Craik to the new see, and
professing to be attested by Chad and Cedd ; but the
fingers of the two saintly brothers had long mouldered in
the dust, when that pious deed was signed.†

As is the case with much of Christian work, there are
but few outward memorials of Chad's labours in the northern

---

* Simeon of Durham in Twysden's Decem Scriptores, Col. 68. Ibid Col. 68.
† The deed professes to be executed in the pontificate of Agatho, but Chad was not
made bishop of Lichfield until after that pontiff's decease.

diocese. No stately fabric records his munificence as an ecclesiastic, or bears silent witness to his genius as an architect.

Even the basilican Church which had been erected by Paulinus, and which had fallen into a state of great dilapidation it was reserved for his successor to restore. The Scottish clergy for the most part had been content to build their churches of wood, and it was one of the features which relieved the Roman proclivities of Wilfrid, that he taught his countrymen to admire and to imitate the worthier architecture which surrounded the Capitol.

Building at all events was not Chad's forte; his work was rather with the hearts of living men. The fierce Thegns and Ealdormen, who surrounded the throne of Oswy, found in the humble bishop a will as firm, and a courage of as true a metal as their own. The new evangel which he preached amid the wolds and dales of Deira threw its shield over the virtue of women, and stirred in the heart of the captive thrall the echo of a forgotten brotherhood. The rough Franklin recognised in the holy man who crossed, barefooted, his threshold, in his hand the volume of mysterious lore, a kind and sympathising friend, almost a visitant from a brighter and better world. For such work of love earth can offer no meet reward. But the cup of cold water given in the name of a disciple will one day be remembered.

The people of the north were not unmindful in later times
of the virtues of their ancient Saint, though their admiration was tinctured by mediæval superstition. Early in the
14th century was founded,* behind the high altar in the
glorious minster which their eyes never beheld, a chantry in
joint honour of Saint Paulinus and Saint Chad, whose virtues were thus blended in the gratitude of posterity. It
was founded and endowed with five marks a year by the
vicars for the soul of John de Burton, rector of Hugate,
and Richard and Alice his parents, in consideration of the
sum of 389 marks which he paid to them. An inventory of
gifts dated 1378 which had been laid upon the altar has
been preserved, and throws light upon the belief of the age.
Amongst other offerings was a missal valued at £4 17s.
11d. a chalice worth £4; a vestment of red satin embroid-
ered with white roses of silk, appraised at £4 16s. 11d.
In a later inventory, dated 1543, the gifts are far less
costly, and mark the decay of faith in the merits of the
Saints and liberality to their shrines ; the list concludes
with "an old blew westment with nothing belonging to
" hit, thre alter clothes upon the alter, one of theyme wth a
" frontlet ; iiij other alter clothes wth one frontlet; ij cruets
" and old towels ; one clothe abowfe the alter and the other
" under the alter ; a pan and a sacrayng bell, a nold laten
" candell styck."

* Vol. of Fabric Rolls published by Surtees Society.

Notwithstanding the decay and contempt into which they afterwards fell, the Chantries were often founded in faith, and were the expression of a feeling which will ever find an echo in the Christian heart. The wish to revere the memory of the departed is one of the most distinguishing and honourable instincts of humanity ; the belief that the grave does not wholly sever the communion between the living and the dead is one of the most consoling which have been engrafted upon the teaching of the Gospel. The hands that placed the silver chalice and the costly missal upon the altar of Saint Chad, for the peace of a departed soul, may have been guided by a faith as genuine, and a heart as pure, as ever prompted a child to light a taper before the image of the Virgin in some silent tomb, or to grace with its wreath of immortelles the grave of a sister sleeping peacefully beneath the willows of Père Lachaise.

Among the many beautiful windows which cast upon the minster floor the quaint forms of departed worthies, limned in "the translucent glass," a place has been found in later times for the first Saxon bishop of the diocese. The silent effigy of the Saint looking down upon us from its stony mullions, will give, at least, as true a notion of what this man was like in the flesh as the curious legends in which a pious fancy has enshrined his memory. The same age, too, which beheld the towers of "stately York," slowly rising aloft in their queenly beauty, beheld generation after generation kneeling upon its rush-strewn. floor, to recite the virtues, and to invoke the intercession of Saint Chad in the language of that wonderful borderland of faith and superstition, the mediæval Breviary.

Nor was Chad forgotten in the noble pile with which the fame of Cuthbert is more immediately connected.* In one of the windows of the Galilee of Durham Cathedral is a portrait of the Saint; † and in the *Liber Vitæ* of their Church his name, amongst those of other northern saints, was written by the monks, as was meet, in letters of gold.

* Dixon's Fasti Eboracenses.   † Ibid.

St CHAD.

FROM THE NORTH AISLE OF CHOIR, YORK MINSTER.

CHAPTER IV

Within his cell,
Round the decaying trunk of human pride,
At morn, and eve, and midnight's silent hour,
Do penitental cogitations cling ;
Like ivy round some ancient elm they twine
In grisly folds and strictures serpentine.

WORDSWORTH.

ON resigning the see he had so ably administered, Chad returned to his beloved monastery of Lastingham, dear to him as the scene of many devout and tranquil hours spent within its walls, and as containing the ashes of the brothers he loved so well. The personal interest he took in the welfare of the brethren would not be lost sight of in his official connection with their monastery. To Lastingham and Lindisfarne he would look for candidates for ordination. They were, so to speak, the Oxford and Cambridge of the north, and long continued to supply the Church with earnest and devoted labourers.

And now that the bishop himself had once more sought its comparative quiet and repose, it would be difficult to set too high a value upon the influence which radiated from that lonely minster. Though Lastingham is now chiefly

I

interesting to the antiquary, history assigns to it no mean place in the annals of English civilization. At the time of its erection, there were but two other Celtic monasteries in the north, and for two hundred years, it was one of the most important centres of religion and learning between the Humber and the Tweed. It was the absence of suitable seminaries at home which filled the monasteries of Ireland and Gaul with English scholars, and eventually led to the foundation of a college for their education at Rome, under the eye of the sovereign pontiff himself.

The monastic orders had not, as yet, adorned the land with their majestic sanctuaries, nor enriched them with the offerings of devotion and superstition. No parish churches, in those early days, reared aloft their spires amid the quiet homes of our forefathers, nor had the " parson " as yet taken up his abode amongst the poor, as their teacher and their friend.

That Theodore and his successors were ever able to divide England into parishes, with a responsible minister of reli- gion assigned to each, was due in no small degree to the previous labours of the few wise master-builders gathered together into the early Celtic and Saxon monasteries, such as Lastingham. For a long time they were but few in number. Lindisfarne was yielding a noble harvest to the labours of Saint Aidan. Saint Hilda had gathered toge- ther her band of high-born maidens, first at Hartlepool, and afterwards at Whitby, where, in later times, on account of her sanctity,

> They told, how sea-fowls' pinions fail
> As over Whitby's towers they sail,
> And sinking down, with flutterings faint
> They do their homage to the Saint.

At Ripon a noble foundation had been laid, but the monks, unwilling to abandon their Celtic traditions, had been superseded by Wilfrid at the head of monks of the Roman party. Further north, amid the winding banks of the Tweed, a succession of devout men was preparing the way for the stately fabric whose "broken arches and shafted oriel" the poet would veil in the dim light of the moon's silvery beams. But the stately aisles of Durham and Hexham had not yet been built, nor did the pale light, at which Bede worked and prayed, as yet, gleam from Yarrow over the rippling waters of the Wear. It would be, probably, not far wrong to say that when Chad returned to Lastingham there were not more than ten centres of religious influence in the whole kingdom of Northumbria.

The monastic life, here pursued, resembled that at Lindisfarne. It was marked by great bodily austerity, combined with fervent zeal in the preaching of the gospel. Great attention was given to the study of the Scriptures. This would be in one of the Latin versions with which the Western Church had been enriched, as Cœdmon had not yet clothed the thoughts of Apostles and Prophets in

his own mother tongue. "There," in short, if we may
apply the words of our gifted countrywoman, "learning
"trimmed her lamp; there contemplation plumed her wing,
"there the traditions of Art, preserved from age to age
"by lonely studious men, kept alive in form and colour
"the idea of a beauty beyond that of earth, of a might
"beyond that of spear and shield, of a divine sympathy
"with suffering humanity."

Chad's devotion to sacred studies is commemorated in
the Breviary :—

> Claustri clausus carcere Cedda monachatur
> At divinis libere vacans his utarur
> Cujus fama claruit quam pontificatur
> Lucerna quae latuit ne plus abscondatur

In the same service his meekness and patience under the
change of worldly fortune are justly commended :—

> R.　Hunc quem magnum reddit autoritas
> 　　Ceddam parvum facit humilitas
> 　　Cui nunquam deest benignitas
> V.　Non attollit illum prosperitas
> 　　Neque frangit quevis adversitas.

Nor is it forgotten how the Saint attained in the cloisters
of Lastingham to the chiefest of all monastic graces :—

> Mundi calcans gloriam
> Cedda declinavit
> Corporis lasciviam
> Dum sese claustravit.

Whatever view now may be taken of monastic institutions, with their puerile discipline and wearisome round of minute observances, one valuable feature cannot be denied to them ; they afforded an excellent opportunity for obtaining seasons of spiritual rest not less needful to the minister of religion than to other men. After his labours in the Northumbrian diocese, Chad doubtless gladly returned to his humble cell. There he rested from one episcopate, and in God's providence prepared to enter upon another. He was a man of far too much ability and character to be passed over in any future episcopal appointments, while the circumstances under which he had resigned the bishopric of York entitled him to the favourable consideration of the Primate. It was not long before an opportunity occurred of shewing a fitting mark of respect to his piety and zeal. The kingdom of Mercia had embraced Christianity under King Peada, son of Penda. His short reign was followed, on the overthrow of the Northumbrian rule, by that of his brother Wulpher, who, notwithstanding the grievous apostacy and murder with which he was afterwards charged, carried out the policy and schemes set on foot by his brother. Since the first establishment of the Mercian see, due amongst others to the labours of Cedd, the brother of our Saint, four bishops had each passed through a brief but toilsome episcopate.

On the death of Jeruman, the fourth bishop, in the year

669, Wulpher applied to Theodore to appoint a successor. The Archbishop had not forgotten the humble-minded man who had so meekly stepped down from the episcopal throne of York, and, with the king's consent, offered him the vacant see of the Mercians. His consecration having been already completed, in what was deemed the canonical manner, he did not need to receive again the episcopal rank, and forthwith entered upon the duties of his diocese. His appointment to the see is curiously described in the * *Life of St. Werburga* in some verses which the reader may like to see.

> Furthermore, after dethe of Jerumanus
> Bysshop of Lychfelde, Wulfer the sayd kynge
> Desyred the archbysshop and prymate Theodorus
> To graunt them a bysshop of holy lyvynge,
> To governe the people by spyrytuall techynge,
> To shew to his subiectes the ensample of vertu,
> And to prech and terche the fayth of Chryst Jhesu.
>
> This holy archbysshop and primate Theodorus
> Desyred Saynt Cedda of the kynge Oswy
> For his perferyon and lyvynge vertuous
> To be removed to the provynce of Mercy.
> Kynge Wulfer was glad of his compynge truly,
> Right so were all the people of his realm,
> Thaukynge therefore the kynge of Jerusalem.

From this account it will be seen that Wulpher applied to his royal contemporary, rather than to the Primate, as

---

* The editor of this curious piece of biography points out the necessity of placing the accent on the last syllable of each line.

stated by Bede. The probability is, that their joint consent was needed, as Chad was at that time residing in the territories of Oswy.

Robert of Gloucester records the same transaction in the metrical life attributed to him.

> After the bishop of the Marsh,* as God it willed was dead,
> The King Wolfer of the Marsh took his red,†
> And into Northumberland his messengers he sent
> To the King Oswy of the land, that he St. Chadde him grant,
> To be bishop of Litchfield, and of all the Marsh also,
> So that as our Lord it willed this deed was ido. ‖

The fame of Chad's piety and zeal had been wafted into Mercia, and no doubt induced the king to desire to have him for the spiritual teacher of his people ; but Wulpher had not forgotten the humble labours of Cedd in the days of his unhappy brother Peada.

With the invitation so flatteringly expressed, Chad thought it right to comply, and accordingly bade farewell to his beloved home at Lastingham and in company with Ovin, his faithful friend, set out for Repton in Derbyshire, where Diuma, the first bishop of the Mercians, had established the episcopal see. At this time there was a monastery of religious men and women established at Repton, and governed by an abbess. It was a place of some importance in Anglo-Saxon times. Here were buried several of the Mercian Kings and here the famous anchorite Saint Guthlac

---

* Mercia. † counsel. ‖ done.

took shelter when he renounced the world. It is still a place distinguished for learning, and more than one eminent scholar owes his education to the Grammar School of Repton.

Whether the new bishop desired a more central place for the episcopal see, or was influenced by the wish to do honour to a spot enriched with the blood of martyrs and confessors, Bede does not tell us, but Chad established the Mercian see at a place then called Licetfeld, or the Field of the Dead. Here perished, according to the tradition, in the fiery persecution of Diocletian, a thousand British Christians with Amphibalus at their head. Be that as it may, Chad removed the see to Lichfield, afterwards the site * of " one of the most complete and beautiful, though not " among the largest of those sacred edifices, which were " raised by the pious hands of our forefathers to the honour " and glory of God."

The early Saxon sees, it should be remembered, were for the most part conterminous with the political kingdoms, owing to the paucity of persons qualified to fill the office of bishop. On this account, the earlier bishops took the titles of their sees from the people to whom they ministered, rather than from the place in which the episcopal chair was established. Thus Chad's correct designation is, bishop of the Mercians, and not bishop of Lichfield. This fact is further illustrated in the varied fortunes of the different

* Gresley's Siege of Lichfield, p. 1.

sees. On the death of Chad, for instance, the Mercian bishopric was divided into the five sees of Lichfield, Leicester, Worcester, Hereford, and Sidnachester. In 786 the see of Lichfield, thus restricted, was raised, through the ambition of Offa, to the metropolitan dignity, of which, however, it was shorn by the Council of Cloveshoe in 803. In the year 1075 the see was removed, by the bishop, to Chester, and fifteen years later, by his successor, to Coventry, and finally, restored to Lichfield by Bishop Clinton.

But to return to the first bishop of Lichfield. In addition to the spiritual oversight of the Mercian kingdom, embracing some twelve thousand families, Chad was desired to take under his episcopal charge the Lindisfari, one of the subordinate communities established by the Saxons, and, at that time, subject to the Mercian crown, with a territory said to be equal to 7000 hides, or about 170 square miles.*

This enormous diocese, comprising no less than seventeen counties, and extending from the banks of the Severn to the shores of the German Ocean, was far beyond the power of one man to administer effectually. In default of anything approaching a parochial system, the bishop could but extend, and guide, as far as possible, the monastic agency. Scattered here and there throughout the country, these communities served as missionary stations, and became the centres of religious life in their respective neighbourhoods. Without

* Stevenson's Bede, p. 443 in Church Historians of England.

K

the preliminary efforts of the monks in breaking up the ground, the parochial system of Theodore would have been premature and useless, nor would a national church have been aught but a dream, if these men had not first gathered its component parts together.

It was upon such help that Chad had mainly to rely. His royal friend, with this view, gave him an estate, equal to the support of fifty families, at a place called At Barwe, in Lincolnshire. It was a place of some note before the time of the Danish invasions, and Bede speaks of the traces of monastic life, established there by Chad, as existing in his time; but the site has not been satisfactorily identified.* It was destroyed, with most of the monasteries of East Anglia and Northumbria, by those ruthless marauders, and the site afterwards granted by King Edgar to Thorney Abbey in Cambridgeshire.

More interesting than the numbers was the nationality of the people, to whom Chad was called to preach the gospel. A great deal has been written about the extermination of the Britons by their Saxon conquerors, but no one can seriously believe that all the Celto-Romano population utterly perished, from out of seventeen counties, even at the edge of the Saxon sword. There can be no doubt that the dominant population of his diocese were the Angles, but subject to them, in a variety of subordinate positions,

---

* Barton-on-Humber and Barrow, near Goxhill, have been suggested.

were the vanquished inhabitants, whose forefathers the legions of Honorius had left to the mercy of succeeding conquerors. The former section of the population spoke the mother-tongue of Saint Chad, and with the latter, his knowledge of the provincial Latin, and of the Celtic tongue acquired in Ireland, enabled him to maintain a precarious, if not satisfactory, communication. The Angles are said to have been less fierce than the Saxons, but the enemies with which the gospel had to contend in Mercia, were formidable enough. It could have been no easy task to persuade the conquered Briton to forget the sea of blood through which the Mercian kings had waded to their throne, and to kneel in the same Church with the haughty conquerors who regarded him as their slave. Ages passed away before these unhappy memories were effaced; and the two great races, which met on the soil of Britain, yielding to the softening influences of time and religion, sheathed the sword, thenceforth only to draw it against the foes of their common fatherland.

Yet, looking at the nature of the gospel itself, we may well believe that the embers of provincial Christianity, in Mercia, were not utterly extinguished by the Angles. During the heat of struggle and conquest, the influence from this quarter may have been scarcely appreciable, but it insensibly allied itself with the better aspirations of the pagan mind, and helped to prepare the ground upon which the seed, sown by Chad and his successors, afterwards fell.

But had the voice of the ancient British Church been for ever hushed, the Teuton myths themselves silently pleaded the cause of the Gospel. Those who have studied them minutely, have discerned many interesting affinities, between these now forgotten fables and the Christian system, which at least facilitated the transition from paganism.*

Not less powerful than these positive influences on the side of the Celtic Missionary, was one of a negative and destructive character. For ages, a disintegrating process had been acting upon the varied forms of Aryan paganism, before which many of its most ancient beliefs are even now crumbling into ruins. A mighty famine arose in the dim and shadowy realm of the pagan religion, and many a wanderer, weary of the empty husks of debasing superstition, listened, gladly, to a gospel which promised to clothe the penitent sinner with the best robe in his heavenly Father's house. The issue could not long be doubtful between the Edda and Voluspa which gave but a stone, and the gospel that offered the Living Bread which came down from heaven.

If the reader would measure, with scrupulous accuracy, the value of Chad's personal efforts in the spread of Christianity in England, it must be sought in the moral, rather than in the intellectual sphere of operation. His lot

* Some interesting remarks on this subject will be found in the preface to Dr. Moberley's new edition of Bede ; see, also, "the Conversion of the Northern Nations," by Dr. Merivale, who exhibits, in a very interesting manner, the moral characteristics of the Teuton race, and the nature of the soil upon which the Gospel seed fell.

was cast in one of the least enlightened of what have been called the 'ages of faith.' The age which conceived, supplies the antidote to the irony. Knowledge and credulity, alike remote from Christian faith, advance in ever-widening but concentric circles, but the relation between them, being inherent in human nature, does not appreciably vary from generation to generation. Without disparagement, therefore, to the Celtic missionaries, it may be freely admitted that their work was rather to subdue stubborn wills, than to reconcile subtle intellects, to lead warriors, rather than philosophers, to the cross of Christ. From this point of view, the austerities which, to us, seem absurd, were not without a powerful moral effect upon the more sensual aspects of the Teuton character. The prelate who was stript of rank and dignity, without a murmur, set a beautiful example of Christian meekness, to men, with whom anger was a grace, and revenge a virtue. The bishop, and friend of kings, who visited, on foot, the hut of the humblest thrall in his diocese, could not fail to commend and adorn the Gospel he proclaimed. So, at least, his merits were regarded in later times :—

This holy man forced himself as he ever did before,
To preach to the folk of Jesus Christ that souls should not be lost.
On his bare feet, as he did before, about he wended there,
The men, for his humility, the more believing were.

But however needful and meritorious were Chad's individual exertions, he well knew that he must provide for the future instruction of his flock.   He therefore gathered together a small college of students in a monastery which he built in Lichfield.   One of these succeeded him in the bishopric, another was Saint Ovin, of whom mention has already been made.

Besides the monastery, there was a church dedicated to Saint Mary, which, in the absence of any statement to the contrary, must be presumed to have been already in existence when Chad entered upon the diocese, and if not a relic of early British Christianity, was probably erected by one of his predecessors in the see.

Hardly less important than the internal administration of his diocese, was Chad's position in relation to the see of Rome.   He had been consecrated by a bishop of the Roman communion, deposed from his bishopric by the primate Theodore, and reconsecrated by him according to the Roman ritual.   But neither of these transactions necessarily compromised his position as a bishop of the Anglo-Saxon church.   Neither the British nor English church, had ever renounced communion with Rome, and consequently Chad's consecration, by Wini, could in no way be construed into an admission of Roman supremacy.   Archbishop Theodore, it will be remembered, had been commissioned to England *in compliance with the invitation* of the kings of Northumbria and Kent, and it was simply by an abuse of his power as metropolitan, that Chad had been

deprived of his bishopric. That he submitted to be reconsecrated, was not from any submission to Roman authority
or jurisdiction which our forefathers would have spurned,
but from a laudable desire to comply with catholic usage.

Yet it cannot be denied that a deep debt of filial gratitude
was due to the see of Rome. Civilization and learning
had followed in the train of her missionaries, and numerous
seminaries attested their indefatigable zeal. Gathering up,
into their own hands, the various elements of civil supremacy, they paved the way for the union of the petty
kingdoms under one political sceptre. But the gospel
blessing had not as yet been reversed ; the son had not yet
been reduced to the rank of a servant, nor filial gratitude
interpreted to mean perpetual bondage. The Bretwalda
of the Confederation, had, for a while, acquiesced in the
views of Wilfrid and his party, but his subsequent policy
in appointing Chad to his see, showed, that the shadow of
Roman authority was creeping but slowly over the face of
English statesmanship.

In his first episcopate, Chad represented an ecclesiastical
system without the pale of the Roman hierarchy, but by the
time he entered upon the bishopric of the Mercians, Roman
influence was making rapid strides. The Celtic missionaries,
wandering from the green shores of Ireland, had carried
the gospel almost to the gates of Rome herself, but were
now, in their turn, met at every point by monks of the

coronal tonsure.　The history of Chad's own mission to the Mercian kingdom might seem to identify him entirely with the Roman party, but one or two considerations may serve to correct this impression, and to disclose his real ecclesiastical position.　In the first place, Rome was not then, what she has since grown to be.　Her claims to universal supremacy, though loudly asserted, had not been recognised by the Churches of the West.　The theology of the Vatican differed, but little, from that studied at Iona and Lindisfarne.　The sword of Infallibility, recently unsheathed before the dazzled gaze of Christendom, was then resting in its scabbard.　The questions, which have since rent the unity, and disturbed the peace of the western Church, had not arisen.　Hence it is plain that Chad, or any other Bishop of his time, might comply with what seemed the more catholic and apostolic usages of Rome, without in the least degree compromising the independent and local rights of his Church.　Saint Chad's predecessors in the Mercian see had been exclusively of the Celtic school, but he himself may fairly be taken to represent that spirit of catholic patriotism, and practical wisdom, which has alternately exposed our Church to the scorn of papists and puritans, but has enabled her to be the dispenser of grace and comfort, to successive generations, and to preserve an unbroken continuity, amid the vicissitudes of successive conquests, through the painful process of needful reformation, and the more violent storms of ungodly revolution, and civil strife. He was actuated by the self-same spirit of wise toleration, which in later times animated the most successful of the Reformers, and conceived the noble Preface to the book of Common Prayer. Hence Saint Chad, in spite of his consecration by Archbishop Theodore, and his subsequent canonization, is to be regarded as the prelate of a church which accepted the friendly offices of, and maintained filial relations with, the see of Rome, but still retained its independence and administered its own affairs.

But the questions which have given rise to these reflections were hardly within the scope of the controversies of Chad's time. His own forte was not in arguing about the Gospel, or in contending for earthly rank, but in preaching it to the poor and winning his way into their hearts by humility and charity. Remote in heart, as in place, from the storms which were agitating the diocese he had so humbly quitted, he pursued the quiet and earnest work of the Christian bishop; studying very devoutly and diligently the Scriptures, out of which he was to instruct his flock, and gathering round him earnest spirits to help and succeed him in his Apostolic labours.

Like all truly devout men, he set little store upon external aids, apart from communion with, and help from God. Knowing the value and need of prayer, he erected for

L

himself a cell, by the side of a fountain, in Lichfield, where he spent many hours alone with God, and so prepared himself to labour for the good of man.　Legend has been busy with both fountain and cell; but, the soberest truth and the humblest faith, trace much of the progress of the Gospel in Britain to the prayers offered in these sequestered oratories.

CHAPTER V.

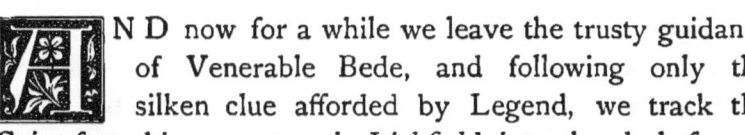 N D now for a while we leave the trusty guidance of Venerable Bede, and following only the silken clue afforded by Legend, we track the Saint from his monastery in Lichfield into the dark forests of Mercia, where, after the manner of holy men of his time, he had built a little cell or oratory. Here, we are told, choosing for himself the better part of Mary, and desiring to devote himself to prayer and meditation, he led for a while a hermit's life. His cell was built upon a grassy bank amid the thick foliage of the forest trees, and on the margin of a clear fountain, at whose refreshing waters he was wont to quench his thirst, and with the roots of herbs and the fruits of woodland trees to satisfy his hunger.

At this time, Wulpher, son of the renouned king, Penda the Strenuous, ruled over the Mercians, and had been hailed as Bretwalda of all the Angles and Saxons. He had espoused the beautiful Ermenilda, a daughter of the

L 2

royal house of Kent, and descended from the noblest stock
of the Franks.   Though fair in form and lineage, she was
accounted fairer still in faith and sanctity.   In due time she
bore to the king four fair children ; three sons, Wulfade,
Rufine, and Kenred, and one daughter, the beauteous
Werburga.   The boys are said to have been adorned with
all princely graces, and to have excelled in all the manly
exercises suited to their rank.   The courtesy of their
demeanour, the prudence of their conduct, and the wit of
their conversation, endeared them to their father's subjects,
both rich and poor.   But their sister, Werburga, had early
been dedicated by the queen, her mother, as a chaste virgin
to Christ ; wherefore, says the chronicler, " thinking scorn of
her royal wooers, and recoiling from the pompous splendour
and pride of all worldly glory, as a violet, she bloomed in
the beauty of unsullied youth, and, as a lily, adorned the
garden of the Lord in the brightness of her virgin purity."

Their father, King Wulpher, had been baptized, many
years before, by the holy Bishop Finan, of the nation of the
Scots ; and at the font, and afterwards when he led his
bride to the altar, he made a vow to the Lord that he would
utterly destroy the temples of the demons, and root out the
idols from his realm, and extend, as far as he should be able,
the faith of Jesus Christ.

But, when he inherited the throne of his fathers, he
forgot to perform the vow which he had made, and idolatry

still lingered in the kingdom of the Mercians. In this
wickedness the king was countenanced by one, Werbode,
whom he had made his chief councillor and friend, such as
Haman the Agagite was to King Ahasuerus. They say
that he was an idolater, a man of Belial, a very minister
and satellite of Satan ; that he was crafty in heart, wily in
tongue, wanton in appetite, and arrogant in mind. Not
content with the favours which the king had already
bestowed upon him, he even dared in his heart to think of
wooing the lovely Werburga, well knowing that she was
dedicated to Christ, hoping, in his madness, thereby, to
succeed to the kingdom.

The king, not heeding, consented to Werbode's suit, but
the queen, Ermenilda, sharply rebuked him for his pre-
sumption, and reproached him with his base lineage. And
Werburga, herself, as beseemed a maiden who was soon to
take the veil, bade him think no more of her as his bride,
but rather to seek for God's forgiveness for having conceived
such a thought in his heart. Her brothers, the Princes
Wulfade and Rufine, in more impetuous mood, threatened
him with their sorest vengeance, if ever again he should
prefer his low-born suit to their sister. The disdainful
words of these royal youths rankled in the evil mind of
Werbode, and one day cost them dear, albeit, through the
teaching of holy Chad, they were to earn the crown of
martyrdom, as the story sheweth. For it fell upon a day, as

the holy man was engaged in devout prayer and meditation
in his cell, a hart of great size, and wide-spreading antlers,
burst forth from the forest glades into the open space which
surrounded the fountain. His panting breath, and quivering
limbs, told that the huntsman was on his track, and, to
slake his raging thirst, he began to drink eagerly of the
cooling waters. Pitying the distress of the noble animal,
and moved with the bowels of compassion towards all the
creatures of God, Chad covered him with the boughs and
leaves of trees, to refresh him with their coolness, and to
conceal him from his foes, for in his inward mind he believed
something wonderful would happen by means of the hart.
And, when the animal was somewhat recovered, it meekly
suffered the holy man to put a cord round its neck, and
then it wandered into the forest to crop the grass.

Hardly had the saint recovered from the surprise
occasioned by the appearance of the hart, than the blast of
a hunter's horn fell upon his ear, and soon a handsome
youth, in gay apparel, reined in his steed in front of the
cell, whither the footprints of the hart had guided him.
This was no other than Wulfade, the king's eldest son, who
had been following the chase—to which, as became one of
royal lineage, he was much addicted—and, in the eagerness
of his pursuit, had lost sight of his retainers.

On seeing the holy man, who, at the sound of the horse's
footsteps, had come out of his cell, the prince courteously

and reverently saluted him, and enquired whether he had seen the hart of which he had been in quest since the early dawn. To whom the saint replied, " Am I the keeper of " the hart ? I do not tend or guard the beasts of the forest, " or the cattle of the field, or the birds of the air, but, through " the ministry of the hart, have become the guide of thy " salvation. For God, who prepared the hart, hath made " known to thee the hidden things of His own sacraments, " that thou mayest believe in His name, and be baptized " for the remission of sins. By a beautiful foreshadowing, " nay, by the witness of a sure prophecy, the hart bathed in " the fountain sets forth and shews to thee beforehand the " laver of wholesome baptism, even as thou mayest learn " the mind of David from the text, ' As the hart panteth " ' after the water brooks, so panteth my soul after Thee, " ' O God ; my soul thirsteth for God as the living fountain, " ' when shall I come and appear before God.' "

Many other things, also, did the saint set forth, shewing him how that by the ministry of irrational animals the Divine Wisdom had deigned to reveal His own mysteries for the salvation of the faithful. By means of a dove, He announced to Noah, after the flood, that the waters, which had covered the earth, were dried up. By the mouth of a lowly ass He restrained the madness of the prophet, and by the ministry of a raven fed the prophet Elijah. And the Lord, Himself, after the custom of the prophets, when He

made His entry into Jerusalem, deigned to ride on an ass
and her colt, in token of the conversion of two peoples.
Nor did he forget to tell him what is read of the blessed
Eustachius, how the Lord vouchsafed to appear to him in
the form of a stag; and many miracles of brute animals
which have been accomplished, and which are found written
in the Acts of the blessed Martin and Jérome.

The prince is related to have replied in all courtesy to
the words of the holy priest " Truly, O reverend father,
" these testimonies might well be believed, even if they
" rested on your sanctity alone; but for my part the things
" which you tell me would be more likely to work faith in
" me, if the animal which I have been pursuing which you
" have hidden by the fountain, and have taught to wander
" in the forest with a rope round its neck, should appear
" forthwith in our presence, in answer to your prayers or in
" obedience to your command."

Straightway the holy priest prostrated himself in prayer.
And lo! the hart aforesaid, bearing the cord upon his neck,
burst forth from the forest and stood before them.   Then
quoth the Saint rising from his knees " Understand now in
" truth that all things are possible to him that believeth, and
" if any one shall ask the Father anything, in the name of
" the Son, it shall be done unto him.   Hear therefore O my
" son and see; incline thine ear to obey the faith of Christ,
" to receive the grace of baptism, for according to the

" promise of our Saviour, ' he who believeth and is baptized
" shall be saved.' "

Comforted and strengthened in the faith, Wulfade threw
himself at the feet of the man of God, and prayed that he
might forthwith be baptized. The blessed Chad, seeing him
thus rooted and grounded in the faith, returned thanks to
God, and, as was meet, first began to instruct him in the
rudiments of the religion of Christ. Then, having solemnly
blessed the fountain, he baptized him therein in the name of
the Holy Trinity, and became, so to speak, his spiritual
father.

And since evening was coming on apace, and day was
now fast declining, the holy father made his son spend the
night with him, and setting before him such frugal fare as
his cell afforded, entertained him with his devout conversation and instruction. At the same time was seen a thing
wonderful to behold; for just as the holy Chad abode with
the prince, so the hart stood by the side of his steed, the
wild animal with the tame, and laid down beside him in all
gentleness and cropped the green sward.

At early dawn the holy priest celebrated mass and
admitted his youthful disciple to the body and blood of our
Lord, as a true and lively member of His church.

Wulfade, being now entered upon the way of truth, was
troubled for the salvation of his brother Rufine, and
earnestly besought Saint Chad that he would pray to God

M

to incline his heart to embrace the Christian faith. To whom the saint is related, in sterner mood, to have replied, " Why dost thou ask for that to be done by me, which am " of little esteem, which thou mayest obtain from God in a " moment. For thy faith shall bring about thy brother's " salvation, and within the space of three days shall bring " him to the knowledge of the truth; for He who hath " separated you from your mother's womb, will call you " both, by His grace, to Himself; He will justify you in " Himself, He will glorify you from Himself."

Upon this, Wulfade bade farewell to the man of God, and saluted him with a holy kiss, and when he had asked, and received, his blessing, departed to his own home strong in the faith?

On drawing near to his father's house, he met his brother Rufine, who rejoiced greatly to see him, deeming that some evil had befallen him; to whom he related all that had taken place in the forest with the man of God, and earnestly exhorted him to do the like. Rufine heard these things gladly, declaring that he had long been minded to come to the faith of Christ, concerning Whom he had first heard the words of life from Saint Germanus, bishop of the East Saxons. For that holy bishop had come to those parts with the saintly Ermenilda, and living there a long time, had preached the gospel unto many.

The two princes, thereupon, resolved to visit, once more,

the man of God, and that they might carry out their design more prudently, set out early in the morning, leaving the usual track in order to conceal their purpose from the thegns who rode with them. They had not gone far into the forest, when lo ! the hart which had appeared first to Saint Wulfade, having his neck still girt with the cord, shewed himself to them, and led the way to the dwelling of the man of God. Rufine followed him, in his flight, by his footprints, but Wulfade, knowing what these acts of the dumb animal betokened, essayed to recall him with the blast of his horn, fearing lest the beast should, unwittingly, be slain. But the other, not hearing or understanding, urged on the chase, and arrived first at the cell of the man of God.

And then the hart, as aforetime, plunged into the fountain, to the intent that it might be understood by such token as he could, that he would lead the youth to the laver of life-giving baptism. It was said that the most holy Chad, himself, produced that very fountain from the bosom of the earth, by his prayers, which, even to this day, is called Chad's Well, and possesses the power of healing those who are afflicted with divers diseases.

The man of God, knowing in his mind what was taking place, went forth from his cell into the open air, and with his eyes and hands lifted towards heaven, poured forth his earnest prayers for the salvation of the prince. Whilst the bishop was thus devoutly engaged, Rufine drew near, and, at the first glance, was immediately persuaded in his mind that it was no other than the blessed Chad, of whom he had heard Germanus relate so many and so great things. "Art thou," quoth he, "my lord father Chad, beloved of God and men, whilome the friend of Anna, the most Christian king of the East Saxons, the teacher and guide to salvation of my brother Wulfade?" who answering, "I am," he threw himself at his feet, beseeching him most earnestly to admit him, without delay, to Christian baptism. The good bishop, admiring and loving him in his heart, rejoiced greatly that such devotion glowed in the breast of a youth, albeit he seemed to possess the wisdom of old age.

And when Wulfade presently rode up to them, his face beamed with joy, as he praised the godly desire of his brother to receive holy baptism. Then the holy Chad, with exulting tongue, instructed him as was fitting, and afterwards baptized him in the same fountain, Wulfade holding him after the manner taught by holy Church.

After this, the priest celebrated the sacrament of the Mass, and these newly-made lambs of Christ's flock ascending, as it were, shorn from the font, he sanctified with the holy washing of the Immaculate Lamb, perceiving from manifold tokens that they would go up to Mount Gilead, that is, to the glory of martyrdom. Nor did the holy man forget to instruct them to keep the commandments of God, or to set forth to them the precepts of the divine discipline, for well he knew they would cleanse their way by taking heed thereto, according to God's law.

The newly-converted princes, on parting from the presence of the holy bishop, to return to their own home, earnestly besought him that he would deign to take up his abode nearer to the castle of their father, at Wulpherchester, that they might the more easily profit by his holy counsel and instruction. Their request was pleasing in the eyes of the bishop, and he accordingly removed his cell nearer to the place they desired.

They, themselves, repaired daily to the man of God, to assist him in his sacred duties, and often lingered in the hallowed precincts, and concealed under the pretence of hunting, the profession of the Christian faith which they had embraced.

But the evil heart of Werbode, their father's friend and councillor, was full of enmity against the youths for that they had withstood him in his suit to their sister, Werburga. Wherefore, he stealthily spied out all their ways and doings, and watched for every opportunity of inflaming their father's mind with anger against them. And when he found out, for a certainty, that they had become Christians, and were wont to frequent the oratory for divine worship, and to visit the man of God, he made it his business to inform the king thereof, and by dint of setting before him that the spread

of the faith of Christ in his realm would overthrow the
religion of his forefathers, under which Penda, his royal father,
had been so prosperous and had gained so many victories;
and that, moreover, his two sons, in embracing this faith,
were setting at nought his royal authority, he roused the
king to such a pitch of fury that he swore a fearful oath he
would be revenged upon them.

Accordingly, at the earliest dawn on the following day,
when the darkness was still upon the earth, the king having
girded himself with his sword, set out with this child of
the devil towards the place where the man of God dwelt.
But, knowing full well that he would be unable to restrain
the fierceness of his anger, he bade Werbode go in advance
to herald his approach to his sons, that if perchance he
should find them in the oratory, they might, at least, be so
filled with fear as to betake themselves to flight and con-
cealment.

But this son of darkness had no thought of sparing
the hapless lads. Approaching the little oratory with stealthy
steps, he looked in at the window and saw them prostrate
on the ground, earnestly engaged in prayer. And then,
without making a sound or uttering a word, he returned
secretly to the king, and informed him that his sons continued obstinate in their purpose of adoring Christ, and
that so far from displaying any fear, or shewing any respect
to his royal authority, they reviled him as a blasphemer and
an apostate.

At these lying words of Werbode, the king turned pale with wrath, and burning with the unnatural desire to shed the blood of his sons, advanced with rapid strides to the precincts of the oratory. The saintly youths, when they heard the thunder of the king's voice, were anxious for the safety of their spiritual father, fearing lest in his wrath he should lay violent hands on the most holy Chad himself, the anointed of the Lord. For well they knew that for themselves their father would have naught but stripes and reproaches, notwithstanding they were eager, and prepared in heart to suffer revilings and terrors and sundry kinds of death for the name of Jesus.

But the blessed Chad, knowing, as Solomon says, that as the roaring of a lion so is the wrath of a king, at the earnest entreaties of the young princes, fled from the face of Wulpher and hid himself in the remoter parts of the forest. And this he did not that he in any way feared death, which he rather counted as gain, but he foresaw that worthier fruit would issue to many from the life which had been spared, than if he were to rush upon instant death.

King Wulpher, if, indeed, he could be called a king who was neither able nor willing to govern himself, bursting furiously into the chapel, found his sons before the image of the Saviour, earnestly engaged in prayer. Thereupon, he began to heap upon them all manner of reproaches for that they had broken the laws of his realm, and set at nought his authority, and then he fiercely threatened them with his direst vengeance if they did not straightway renounce the faith of Christ, and worship the gods of their fathers.

Then Wulfade, with all Christian meekness and princely dignity, replied that they were most unwilling to break the laws of the land, but that the king had himself once professed the faith which now he renounced; that they earnestly desired to retain his fatherly affection, but that the prospect of no tortures or death could shake their fixed resolve to continue steadfast in the religion of Christ.

But even whilst the brave young prince was yet speaking, the king, fiercer than any wild beast, drawing his sword, rushed furiously upon him and slew him and cut off his head, and consecrated him, all unconscious, a martyr to Christ. The younger, Rufine, seeing these things, fled, but being pursued by his father, received a mortal wound. whereof he presently expired, and, being made a fellow martyr with his brother, departed to celestial glory. And so it came to pass that those whom nature made one on earth, being united in faith and love, were made one also in heaven.

When this horrid crime had been wrought, the king and Werbode turned away with hurried steps from the place which was conscious of his crime. But lest the fell deed should come to the knowledge of the queen or of the people, they agreed to destroy the oratory of the man of God

during the darkness of the night, and to bury the bodies of
the slaughtered princes in some secret place.

But their evil deeds could not long remain undiscovered.
The avenger was at hand. For when the king returned,
with his wicked councillor, to the castle, and had repaired
alone to his own chamber, an evil spirit, at the very entrance
of the royal palace, in the sight of many persons standing
by, seized the schemer of the death of the martyred princes
as his own familiar and vassal. For he straightway began to
tear his hands and arms with his teeth ; and what, at his
own wicked instigation, the blood-stained father had wrought
upon his sons, he, shouting with unrestrained voice, proclaimed in the ears of all men. And, for long, the avenging
demon ceased not to torment him, until at last he forced
him to breathe forth his baleful spirit.

The report of the horrid deed filled all men with sorrow
and amazement, and, when it reached the queen's ears, a
sword of unspeakable grief pierced her soul. Repairing to
the place of her sons' martyrdom, she took up their bodies
and gave them honorable burial in one stone tomb. And,
from that time, the queen resolved to forsake the couch of
her husband, and with her daughter, Werburga, who had
been the unwitting cause of her brothers' death, at length
retired to the monastery of Sheppey, and afterwards to that
of Ely, where she died, after many deeds of piety, in the
odour of sanctity.

N

Meanwhile, the king, overwhelmed with unavailing remorse, took to his bed, and was like to die. To assuage the intolerable anguish of his mind, his friends counselled him to seek solace in hunting, or in falconry, or in instruments of music. But the queen and her kinsfolk admonished him, above all things, not to despair of the divine mercy, but rather to take counsel of the holy bishops, Jaruman and Chad, and to do what, in their judgment, should be meet.

The king yielded to this wiser counsel, and firmly resolved to repair to the holy Chad, and to do whatsoever he should enjoin. Accordingly, one morning he set out with his thegns, as if to follow the chase, hoping to fall in with the man of God by a chance similar to that which had befallen his sons, now, alas! martyrs. For the blessed Chad, immediately after the murder of the saintly youths, had returned to his former dwelling place, by the fountain, and was leading there a hermit life, without a single companion to relieve the dreariness of his solitude.

When the king had advanced into the thicker parts of the forest, and all his attendants, as God willed, were scattered hither and thither, and he was left alone, he espied the meek hart, so often mentioned, bounding in the distance, and having the cord round its neck as aforetime. At sight whereof, being filled with joy, he followed in his track, until, in sooth, he came to the dwelling of the servant of God, the holy Chad. The hart, as though he had finished his errand, left the king, and plunged into the fountain, as he was wont, to cool and refresh himself.

The king immediately dismounted from his steed, and, approaching the window of the oratory, saw the man of God, arrayed in his priestly vestments, standing before the altar, and celebrating mass. Being let by a guilty conscience, he stood within the porch, and durst not enter, until he had first been shriven from his sins by the holy bishop. And, when the bishop began the canon, so great a light shone forth from heaven, through the apertures in the wall, that priest and sacrifice, and all that appertained thereto, were covered with the splendour that was shed upon them. The eyes of the king were blinded with the brightness of the light, for, in comparison with this heavenly radiance, the noon-day sun itself seemed poor and mean. And, marvellous to relate, the splendour in no degree waxed dim until the celebration of the holy mass was accomplished, and then the light departed heavenwards, and the natural sun, entering in at windows and door, darted his rays even to the altar. The holy man knew that the king was standing without, and what it was that he desired in his mind, for the heavenly light shone upon him spiritually as well as corporeally. And, when the sacred office was finished, he hastily put off his priestly vestments, and, thinking to lay them upon the place appointed for them by the side of the altar, unwittingly hung them upon a sunbeam, and went to the king, who was outside the oratory. But the sunbeam upheld the sacred robes, which had been laid upon it, so that they did not fall to the ground, showing, by a manifest miracle, saith the chronicler, that this son of light clave firmly to the Sun of Righteousness by faith and love.

The saint, on going forth, found the king prostrate upon the earth before the porch of the Church, overwhelmed with confusion, on account of his sin, and oppressed with intolerable anguish of mind. The bishop raised him up, and, after the example of the Good Samaritan, poured into the wounds of his mind the oil of consolation, mingled with the wine of sharp reproof, lest he should fall into the sin of despair. "Oftentimes," quoth he, "since that evil day, have I implored the most merciful Creator of all things that he would vouchsafe to take away thy sin, which thou hast committed against thy sons, at the instigation of the minister of death, who has already become an inhabitant of hell. And the Lord, that he might shew to thee the riches of His goodness, hath granted to thee the opportunity of repentance, in answer to my prayers, if thou art willing to follow my counsels."

The king replied, with great humility, that he was willing, in all things, to be guided by his advice, and, in accordance therewith, to make amends for the evil deed which he had wrought.

Wherefore, Saint Chad enjoined upon King Wulpher,

under the seal of penance, that he should, with all speed, cause, by a public edict, all the shrines of the demons to be utterly destroyed throughout the realm of the Mercians; that he should give command to root out idolatry, to build churches, to found monasteries, to ordain clergy, and strictly to observe the ordinances of the Christian religion; he further admonished him that he should do justice between man and man; to devote himself to frequent prayers, to make amends for his sins with works of mercy, according to the exhortation of holy Scripture; to refrain from all corrupt actions, and to be faithful to the marriage bed.

When the man of God had spoken these, and similar, things, he turned a little on one side, and gave himself to prayer, and motioned to the now penitent king that he also should seek the face of the Lord. And Wulpher, chancing to lift up his eyes, saw the priestly vestments hanging upon the sunbeam not without great wonder. Whereupon, he rose from his knees, and approached nearer, that he might see this great vision, and placed his own gloves and baldric upon the beam, but they immediately fell to the ground.

Being now a man of deeper insight, he understood that Saint Chad was accounted the fellow and companion of the saints above, and beloved by the Sun of Righteousness, to whom, whilst living on earth, the sun paid such homage. When, after a little space, the holy bishop ceased praying, the king bade him behold the wonderful sight he had seen.

Then the bishop, drawing near, took up his vestments, and, laying them upon the altar, returned devout thanks and worship to Him who lighteth every man that cometh into the world.

The king, edified, and rejoicing in the Lord, took with him the holy bishop, and returned to his own home and kindred. In short, he laboured diligently to accomplish what he had openly vowed to God, in the presence of His servant. By the advice of the blessed Chad, and with the help of the saintly Ermenilda, within a brief space of time, the king utterly purged his realm from the contamination of idolatry; and, whatever could be thought contrary to wholesome faith, he made it his care to remove. He built, or caused to be built, churches in suitable places; he erected many beautiful monasteries, for both sexes, and enriched them with ample revenues; amongst others, he endowed with many lands and possessions the noble monastery of Medehampstede, which he is said to have founded in order to expiate the crime committed against his sons. In our time, concludes the chronicler, it is called Peterborough, that is, the city of Saint Peter. For the church, which was dedicated in this place in honour of the chief of the Apostles, contains the ashes of many saints, and still sends forth many good men to the holy fellowship of the citizens above; the most blessed Peter conducting them thither, and opening, for them, the gate of the kingdom of heaven.

CHAPTER VI.

Under an oak, whose antique root peeps out
Upon the brook that brawls along this wood :
To the which place a poor sequestered stag,
That from the hunter's aim had ta'en a hurt,
Did come to languish ;

As You Like It.

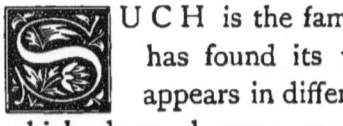 U C H is the famous legend of Saint Chad which has found its way into English literature. It appears in different writings, under various forms, which demand some consideration, as bearing upon any shadow of a claim to be regarded as historical, which might be set up for it.

In the foregoing recital, we have mainly followed the Latin version of the story, printed in the Monasticon, from a manuscript preserved in the Cottonian Library, in the British Museum, which differs but slightly from one in the Fitzwilliam collection, said to have belonged, originally, to the monastery of Peterborough. The writer complains of the barbarous and uncouth language in which the story had hitherto been told, and which had served rather to bring it into contempt, than to tend to edification. He probably refers to the legend as it formerly appeared in the cloister windows of Peterborough minster. The quaint couplets of this version are, however, far more interesting than the bombastic latinity which the monkish scribe supposed to be an improvement.   Each window contained a picture of one of the personages mentioned in the poem, with an explanatory couplet beneath it, the whole series purporting to be a history of the minster from its foundation to the time of King Edgar.   The cloisters were destroyed by the puritan rabble of Cromwell's time, but the legend has been preserved and printed as follows :—

King Penda, a Paynim, as writing septh,
Gate pese five children of Christen septh.

The noble king, Penda, by God's grace,
Was the first founder of this place.

By Queen Ermenyld had King Wulfere
These twey sons that ye see here.

Wulfade rideth, as he was wont,
Into the forest the hart to hunt.

For all his men, Wulfade is gone,
And supth, himself, the hart alone.

The hart brought Wulfade to a well
That was beside Seynt Chaddys cell.

Wulfade asked of Seynt Chad
Where is the hart that me hath led.

The hart that hither thee hath brought,
Is sent by Christ that thee hath bought.

Wulfade prayd Chad that ghostly Leech
The faith of Christ him for to teach.

Seynt Chad teacheth Wulfade the feyth,
And words of baptism over him he seyth.

Saint Chad devoutly to Mass him dight,
And hoseled Wulfade Christys knight.

Wulfade wished Seynt Chad that day
For his brother Rufine to pray.

Wulfade told his brother Rufine
That he was Christened by Chaddy's doctrine.

Rufine to Wulfade said again
Christened also would I be fain.

Wulfade Rufine to Seynt Chad leadeth,
And Chad with love of faith him feedeth.

Rufine is Christened of Seynt Chaddys,
And Wulfade his brother his godfather is.

Werbode, steward to King Wulfere,
Told that his sons Christened were.

Toward the chappel Wulfere gan goe,
By guiding of Werbode, Christys foe.

Into the chappel entred the king
And found his sons worshipping.

Wulfere in woodness his sword out drew
And both his sons, anon, he slew.

O

King Wulfere with Werbode woo,
Wurping gave his sons two.

Werbode for vengeance his own flesh tare,
The devil him strangled and to hell bare.

Wulfere for sorrow, anon, was sick,
In bed he lay a dead man like.

Seynt Ermenyld, that blessed Queen,
Counselled Wulfere to shrive him cleen.

Wulfere, contrite, hyed him to Chad,
As Ermenyld him counselled had.

Chad bade Wulfere for his sin
Abbeys to build his realm within.

Wulfere in haste performed than
Brough that Peada his brother began.

Wulfere endued with high devotion
The Abbey of Brough with great possession.

The third brother, King Ethelred,
Confirmed both his brethren's deed.

Saxulf, that here first Abbat was,
For Ankerys at Thorney made a place.

After came Danes and Brough brent,
And slew the Monkys as they went.

Fourscore years and sixteen
Stood Brough destroyed by Danes teen.

Seynt Athelwold was bidden by God's lore
The Abbey of Brough again to restore.

Seynt Athelwold to King Edgar went
And prayed him to help him in his intent.

Edgar bade Athelwold the work begin
And him to help he would not lyn.

Thus Edgar and Athelwold restored this place,
God save it and keep it for his grace.

The version of the cloister legend printed by the learned
author of the Monasticon contains two or three couplets in
addition to the preceding, and exhibits several verbal differ-
ences besides. The story, as it appeared in the windows of
the minster, was probably of the same date as the cloisters
it adorned. The history of the abbey is brought down to
the time of Edgar, but no further, and it is not impossible
that when the cloisters were erected, the story was rendered
into a more modern form and metre, from a still more ancient version preserved in the abbey. There can, at all
events, be little doubt that the legend in its metrical form, is
due to some monk belonging to Peterborough, anxious to
enhance the ancient glory and the present splendour of his
house. But, like most tales, the legend of Chad and Wulpher's sons has lost nothing in travelling. Among the
multifarious treasures rescued by Sir Robert Cotton from
the " spoils of time," is an account of the martyrdom of

Wulfade and Rufine, furnishing some important particulars unknown to the window scribe, and in which Chad's wonder-working powers are more fully developed. From the many references to the Priory of Stone it seems probable that this poem was written by an ecclesiastic of that house, the foundation of which, if the story is to be believed, may be traced to the martyrdom of the Princes. Several of the leaves of this manuscript are defective, but a few lines will give a specimen of the English. The conversion of the princes is thus related :—

> His brothere Ruffyn of hym greate marvell hade,
> And as he wente hym for to seeke
> He mett hapstely the harte so meyke
> That his brothere to the feyth lade,
> And brought also to holy Saynt Chade.
> There he founde his brothere Saynt Wolfade
> Thereof his harte then was full glade
> The tolde hym all then of that rasse
> What wisse Saynt Wolfade cristened was
> And or he wente God sende hym such grace
> That or he wente he was cristened in that place
> Saynt Chade christenede hym hys owne hande
> And hys brothere was hys godfathere thus J understande
> Saynt Chade went to masse then at hys awtere
> And howeslede them bothe there inferre.

A few lines further on we learn that Chad's cell or oratory was

Þre mylle the kynges place fro,
That the to hym myght ofte cumme and goe ;
In the whiche place there as he made his dwellynge
Was greate plenty of trees then growyng
And of the burgenyng of the trees the whiche there was
Borgen towne men callyde that place
And Borstone nowe hit callyde ys.

Their father and his court thought the young princes were following the chase :

But trewely ever more there huntyng
Was to serche for a more godly thyng ;
Yt was all to visett Saynt Chade J wis
To bringe there sowlle to heven blysse.

Then we have some additional particulars respecting the queen which had escaped the researches of the earlier narrator. When she went to take up the bodies of her murdered sons she was comforted by angels from heaven, and

The angels toke up the body of Ruffyn her sone,
And bare it up in the eyre and bade hur after cumme.

The miracle of the sun-beam, of which nothing is said in the cloister legend, now appears,

The kyng withe great contreepone went to Saynt Chade
For to amende hym of hys lyffe that he evyll hade lade.
When he came to the chapell thereas Saynt Chade was,
There he founde hym devowtly stondying at masse ;
A full fewre myrachle he sae throwe goddis grace ;
The sone hit shone throwe an hoole in the same place ;
Sente Chade or he wente to masse he leyde his clothes him fro
The sone beyme trewly helde them from the grounde tho.

One more verse, describing the miracle of the sunbeam, and its effect upon the king, must conclude our extracts from this poem :—

> Then the foresayd kinge and the holy confessour
> Went to theyr prayers in the oratory
> And as the kynge loked up to our Sabyour
> The sayd sacrat vestures he sawe evydently
> Hangynge on the sonne beam full mervelyously
> His globes, his gyrdell the kynge had upon
> Which shortly to ground falled adowne.

> Whereby he perceyved the great holynesse
> Of blessed Saynt Cead and interyor devocyon
> Despred his prayer dayly with meeknesse
> To Almyghty God for his remyssion
> From thens departed with his benedycyon
> Joyfull in his soule towarde his place
> Thankynge God mekely of his great grace

Besides these metrical versions of the legend, there are extant the Latin version already referred to, an abridgement of the same among the Lansdowne MSS.,* and a short account, in the first volume of that marvellous treasure-house of antiquities, Leland's Collectanea. One important variation in the legend must not be overlooked. The hart is sometimes transformed into a milk-white doe, upon whose milk the holy man is said to have lived; but the original authority for this interesting particular I have been unable to discover.

* 436 ff 236.

Taking the legend as it stands, the question naturally arises, is it altogether a creation of fancy, or has it any basis of historical truth? Did the Mercian king lay violent hands upon his own sons? and does the glorious minster, rising above the green meadows of the gently flowing Nene, carry us back in thought to a monarch, prostrate in the presence of a man of God; and whose guilt-haunted soul cannot be shriven until he has washed away his sin in penitential deeds of charity?

The scornful iconoclasm of modern times, which has plucked away so many flowers from the garden of history, has not spared the legends of the saints. Saint Chad has been dealt with long ago. The accomplished Selden rebuked the ingratitude of the Peterborough monks, who proclaimed their ancient founder to the world as an apostate and a murderer. * Other scholars have torn to shreds the arguments by which the historical character of the story was vindicated, and have triumphantly appealed to the silence of history, in proof of the falsehood of legend. I am by no means ambitious of drawing upon myself the keen shafts of ridicule by disputing conclusions which have been so confidently arrived at. But, were I to do so, I should be in by no means contemptible company. The ingenious author of the *Polyolbion*, in the lines which gave rise to Selden's criticism, has no suspicion that he is clothing a fable in verse:

Smith's Bede, App. XVI.

P

Though his unnatural hands succeeding Wulpher stayned
In his own children's blood whom their dear mother had
Confirmed in Christ's belief by that most reverent Chad,
Yet to embrace the faith when after he began,
(For the unnaturalst deed that ere was was done by man)
If possible it were to expiate his guilt,
Here many a goodly house to holy uses built ;
And shee to purge his crime on her own children done
A crowned Queen for him, became a veiled Nun.

*But however contemptously history may treat the Legend of Saint Chad, its dramatic accessories and ethical bearing agree well with the character of those times. The forest life, he is said to have led in Mercia, had been led in the forests of Gaul and Germany by hundreds of saints before him. The monks and anchorites of mediæval times seem to have inherited the sylvan empire of the Druidical priesthood. For their stern souls such a life possessed peculiar fascinations. The gloomy shades of the forest were for them haunted with fantastic terrors, and peopled by unhallowed beings with whom faith alone could grapple. With axe in hand, and a firm reliance on God's goodness in their hearts, they advanced boldly into these woodland solitudes, and, with a courage worthy of knight or crusader, braved their real and imaginary dangers. The blue smoke which curled upwards above the loftiest trees to heaven, often rose for the first time from the hermit's cell, built of trees he had himself hewn down, and surrounded by the plot of land he had with his own hands rescued from his forest domain.

---

* It is easier for me thankfully to acknowledge than accurately to specify my obligations in the following remarks to Montalembert's interesting work, " The Monks of the West."

Surrounded by a tangled maze of almost primeval vegetation, the legend allows us to picture our Saint reciting day after day, in his lonely cell, the solemn offices of the Catholic Church, amid the murmured responses of waving trees; and, as evening shrouds the forest in yet profounder gloom, chanting his lonely vespers with the distant howling of wolves for a chorus, and the song of many birds for an antiphon.

That the wandering huntsman in quest of wild boar or stag should have fallen in with the saint, engaged in these solitary devotions, was not improbable. Such encounters form the staple of many a monkish story and the burden of many a song. That the holy man should have succeeded in taming one of the antlered monarchs of the forest, equally agrees with the traditional aspects of hermit life. The monkish chroniclers love to tell of Saint Calais stroking the sleek sides of his gentle buffalo; of Saint Marculphus sheltering beneath his robe from its pursuers the hare which like our own poet he had taught to regard him as its friend; of Saint Giles having his outstretched hand pierced with the shaft of the royal huntsman aimed, at the hound he had cherished as the companion of his solitude. The birds of the air, and the fish of the sea, were not behind in shewing respect to the saints. They tell of the otters which licked the frozen toes of Saint Cuthbert after his nocturnal orisons in the sea, and of the fishes which listened devoutly to the exhortations of

Saint Anthony, and of the ravens which robbed Saint
Guthlac of his gloves and parchment but brought them
back again in mute homage to his sanctity ! !

That a Saxon prince should have apostatized from the
Christian faith, and murdered his sons ; and in remorse for
his crime have built churches and monasteries would be
only too credible, were it not in this particular instance con-
tradicted by the well ascertained history of the Mercian
king, and of Saint Chad himself.

The story of the sun-beam belongs, of course, to the
realm of pure fable. But myths have an origin as well as
a meaning, and it would not be surprising if this same story
should hereafter be traced, as many others have been, to
the very cradle of Aryan mythology, and the miracle of
Saint Chad prove to have been performed by some far more
ancient seer at the foot of the Himalayas, or on the banks of
the Ganges. At all events Chad had been anticipated in
the miracle by other Saints in the Catholic Church, as, for
instance, by Saint Goar, of Treves and Saint Aicadrus, of
Jumieges ; concerning whose performance the writers of the
Lives of English Saints are not ashamed to write " it is not
to be wondered at if a ray of the sun assumed the hardness
of wood in obedience to the holy man, since to one who
lives in devout intimacy with the Creator, the creature is
subjected to the Creator's will !" *

* Quoted in Wright's Archæological Essay.

So far then, the incidents narrated in the legend may be considered as in harmony with the notions of the age in which they are said to have occurred. There were such persons as hermits, who forsook the world to dwell alone in forests and in caves and fens. They tamed wild animals and cleared away trees, and, as Montalembert points out, rendered the like service to mediæval civilization, fo rwhich, future generations will thank the hardy pioneers of the forests in the far west.

But, when the laborious servant of Christ, whose portrait Bede has so lovingly drawn, is transformed into one of these lonely anchorites, with a gloomy forest for his diocese and its wild denizens for his flock, nothing further is needed to stamp the story with the genuine marks of fiction.

The monks of Lastingham knew nothing of the hermit life of their former Abbot. Daniel, bishop of Winchester, who wrote a life of Saint Chad, and was a literary correspondent of Bede's, gave no hint of it to his illustrious contemporary. The story of Saint Chad, must accordingly be referred to that large class of compositions, which as pious fables or knightly romances have inculcated moral or religious truth, but must not be confounded with history, though they have borrowed her pen and made use of the names of those who have adorned her brightest pages.

But, although the legends of Saint Chad cannot be accepted as literal fact, we need not suppose that they were written with the purpose of deceiving the unlearned. They were rather the chaplet woven hy the hands of posterity round the memory of one to whom Saxon England owed not a little; the unconscious homage of later times to the softening and elevating influence of the Christian faith over the animal lusts which degrade, and the stormy passions which agitate the hearts of sinful men.

But far from us be any close analysis of this beautiful story. Like other stories of the kind, it answered its purpose, and as such it should be respectfully treated. To pursue it further would be to pull the rose, leaf by leaf to pieces; to scatter them to the wind; to destroy their beauty, and to dispel their fragrance.

CHAPTER VII.

Hark ! hark my soul ; Angelic sounds are swelling
  O'er earth's green fields, and ocean's wave-beat shore.
How sweet the truth those blessed strains are telling,
  Of that new life when sin shall be no more.
Angels of Jesus, Angels of light,
  Singing to welcome the pilgrims of the night.

          *   *   *   *   ·   *   *

Angels sing on ! your faithful watches keeping ;
  Sing us sweet fragments of the songs above ;
Till morning's joy shall end the night of weeping,
  And life's long shadows break in cloudless love.
Angels of Jesus, Angels of light,
  Singing to welcome the pilgrims of the night.

                    HYMNS ANCIENT AND MODERN.

T H E story of a human life has never been com-
pletely told. Its curve, to borrow an expression
from the mathematicians, has never been com-
pletely traced. The development of a man's original
mental and moral constitution, · the influence of external
events upon it for good and evil, the subtle causes which
determine the part he plays in the roll of history are
matters which often baffle the keenest scrutiny of the
biographer, and the ignorance of which reduces the noblest
efforts of his science to splendid fragments, like those
mournful columns in churchyards, which tell of a human life
cut short in its prime. For, like the fabled stream of

Helicon which flowed underground, every life is more or less hidden from the eyes of other men, and not until we enter upon the great hereafter, will its course be known and its secrets revealed.

For this reason many lives which abound in stirring and eventful incidents are not really more interesting or instructive than others of which but little is recorded. The key is wanting to unlock their secrets. A theory is required to explain their complex phenomena.

On the other hand the life of many a good man becomes sublime in its very simplicity, and from the grandeur of the principles which it illustrates. When the clouds of legend, which obscure the personality of St. Chad, have all cleared away, and we breathe once more the pure air of authentic history, we are brought face to face with one to whom England owes an almost unacknowledged debt of gratitude, and who contributed not a little to make her what she now is among the nations of the earth. He was not called like Anselm or Becket to a keen struggle with the civil power; nor yet like Cranmer and Ridley to cleanse the national church of the corruptions of ages; neither was it his part to fan into a flame, like the Wesleys and Whitfields of modern times, the almost extinguished embers of spiritual life. The task, to which he set himself, was to plant the christian faith among a race of pagans, and upon an almost virgin soil to sow the seed of its imperishable truths.

It is when we regard the Britain of Chad's time as the crucible in which were fused the elements of a mighty nation, and the fire which moulded them together as the gospel of Christ, that the humblest preacher of this world-subduing faith becomes invested with almost a sacred interest; his face glows in the page of history, like the face of the alchymist at his furnace, with the flame his own zeal has kindled. The simplicity and earnestness of Chad's charac-ter, the magnitude of the work in which he was engaged, the great success which God gave to his efforts, make the brief recital of his life worthy of our attention, and teach a useful lesson, at a time when there is yet a pagan England to be brought to the foot of the Cross. Gladly would we trace the footprints of the Saint, throughout the beautiful kingdom which constituted his bishopric. It would be pleasant to think of him, travelling in his coracle, on the Trent or Severn, to the villages which fringed their banks; to picture him baptizing crowds of converts in their waters; or to join the humble cavalade as it wends its way along the deserted streets of Uriconium, or through the dark forests in which tradition has given him a home. More edifying still, would it be, to have some fragments of those discourses, which clothed the dry bones of Teutonic paganism, with the spiritual life of christianity. But no Luke has recorded his wanderings, or recounted, for the instruction of posterity, his perils and adventures as a christian missionary; and we are forced to content ourselves with the few particulars concerning their illustrious abbot, which the monks of Lastingham furnished to Venerable Bede.

It has already been mentioned that Saint Chad built a small oratory at Lichfield, where he was wont to read and pray with his monks, as often as he had any spare time from the labour and ministry of the word.

So that monk this holy man as God it willed became,
And with seven other brethren the habit of monk took.
A little distance from Litchfield where was his see,
He had made for him a little cell all in privity;
And when he had gone about and preached also,
In that cell he would remain his order for to do.*

It is not easy to say positively whether this little convent was bound by the rule of S. Benedict, so warmly espoused by Wilfrid, or whether it still adhered to the traditions of the grand old Saint of Iona. That the result of the Whitby Synod, favourable as it was to Rome, did not involve the Benedictine rule, is plain from the fact that Rome, then, as now, threw the shield of her protection over various monastic orders. The primate Theodore himself is thought to have been of the order of S. Basil. There was besides, the Celtic rule, and that of S. Augustine. On the whole it seems probable that the impress of Lindisfarne was too deep upon the mind of S. Chad, ever to be effaced,

* To say his Office.

and there is every reason to believe that he died as he had lived, a faithful disciple of Saint Aidan.

The question might here suggest itself, how far the strict observance of any monastic rule was compatible with the active work of a missionary bishop. How could one engaged in preaching the gospel throughout an extensive territory, like the Mercian kingdom, be bound to recite various offices of the Church at certain specified hours? There can be no doubt, that, in modern times, the superior flexibility of the system devised by Ignatius Loyala, gave his followers a great and admitted advantage, in the mission field, over the Franciscans and Dominicans, and other ancient orders. It is fair to suppose that, in the case of the Celtic missionaries, who united the profession of monk with the office of bishop, the vows of the one were not suffered to impede the work of the other.

A specimen of Chad's mode of instructing his disciples is preserved in Bede, and places his simple piety in a very interesting light. 'It is no wonder,' says the historian, 'that he joyfully beheld the day of his death, or rather the day of our Lord, which he had always carefully expected till it came; for notwithstanding his many merits of continence, humility, teaching, prayers, voluntary poverty, and other virtues, he was so full of the fear of God, so mindful of his last end in all his actions, that, (as I was informed by one of the brethren, who instructed me in the Scriptures, and who had been bred in his monastery, and under his direction, whose name was Trumbert) if it happened that there blew a stronger gust of wind than usual, when he was reading or doing any other thing, he immediately called upon God for mercy, and begged it might be extended to all mankind. If the wind grew stronger, he closed his book, and prostrating himself on the ground, prayed still more earnestly. But if it proved a violent storm of wind or rain, or else that the earth and air were terrified with thunder and lightning, he would repair to the church, and devote himself to earnest prayers, and the repeating of psalms, till the weather became calm. Being asked by his followers why he did so, he answered, " Have you not read, The Lord also thundered from the heavens, and the Highest gave forth His voice. Yea He sent out His arrows and scattered them, and He multiplied lightnings and discomfited them. For the Lord moves the air, raises the winds, darts lightning, and thunders from heaven, to excite the inhabitants of the earth to fear Him ; to put them in mind of the future judgment; to dispel their pride, and to vanquish their boldness, by bringing into their thoughts that dreadful time, when the heavens and the earth being in a flame, He will come in the clouds, with great power and majesty, to jndge the quick and the dead." " Wherefore " said he, " it behoves us to answer His heavenly admonition with due fear and love ; that as often as He lifts His hand through the trembling sky, as it were, to strike, but does not yet let it fall, we may immediately implore His mercy; and searching the recesses of our hearts, and cleansing away the rubbish of our vices, we may carefully behave ourselves so as never to be struck."

Bede's interesting recital is faithfully reproduced in the metrical life :—

When this holy man saw that the weather was overcast,
I have not heard of any man that so sorely was aghast.
When it thundered or lightened he knew not where to be,
But as a man to seek help, to the Church he would flee.
And before he had got there, he durst nowhere tarry,
And there he would cry on God, that the weather might abate.
Such dread he had each time, of lightning and thunder,
As that they who dwelt near him were thereof in wonder.
So that some men one day asked why it were,
And why, more than other men, he should be in such fear.
'Ye fools,' quoth this holy man, 'little know ye what ye see here,
'Nor read ye not what St. David saith in his psalter,
'That our Lord thunders from heaven, and he that highest is
'Gave forth his voice and sent about his arrows I wis.
'The thunder is our Lord's trumpet, and his blow also,
'Then he threateneth for to smite, but we know not when he will do (so).
'Lightnings are his arrows that fly about wide,
'That wonder it is when they fly (about) that man dare anywhere abide.
'He sends them oft for to smite and for to threaten oft,
'To shew men when he smites that his blow is not soft.
'And that men should have in their mind the mighty day of doom,
'For his blow will then be strong enow as we ought to preach lome.'*

* Frequently.

Well ought we sinful men of such weather to have dread,
When this holy man had, who was of such hold deed.

" If this religious man," writes Jeremy Taylor, with
reference to Chad's pious custom, "had seen Tullus
Hostilius, the Roman king, and Anastasius, a Christian
emperor, but reputed heretic, struck dead with thunderbolts,
and their own houses made their urns to keep their ashes
in, there would have been no posture humble enough, no
prayers devout enough, no place holy enough, nothing
sufficiently expressive of his fear and his humility, of his
adoration and religion to the Almighty and Infinite power
and glorious mercy of God, sending out his emissaries to
denounce war with designs of peace."

But Chad's pious and laborious career was rapidly drawing
to a close ; his holy life was to be crowned by a glorious
death.   His episcopate of York had been cut short, but he
was sooner still to be separated from his Mercian flock.
But a man's usefulness to the Church cannot be measured
by any mere unit of time ; a bishop, who laboured after the
fashion of Chad, would do more to spread the Gospel in
three years, than the luxurious prelates of later times would
in half a century of worldly pomp and luxury.

" The divine providence so ordaining," says Bede, "there
came round a season like that of which Ecclesiastes says,—
' That there is a time to cast stones and a time to gather
them,' for there happened a mortality, sent from heaven,

which, by means of the death of the flesh, translated the stones of the Church from their earthly places to the heavenly building." Supernatural intimations of his approaching departure are said to have been vouchsafed to the bishop. For, when the hour of his death drew near, it chanced one day he was in the little oratory, which he had built, engaged in study and prayer. Not far off, his faithful friend Ovin, was busily employed out of doors, for the monks of those days thought no scorn of manual labour so that it was for the glory of God. As he laboured, suddenly the sound of voices, of surpassing sweetness, fell upon his ear, as of persons singing and rejoicing, and as though they were descending slowly from heaven to earth. No vision met his gaze, but, as he listened with rapt attention, the celestial music, which, at the first, seemed to come from the south east, now hovered nearer to him, and, at length, passing through the roof of the oratory, where the bishop prayed, for the space of half an hour filled the building with its glorious strains ; then Ovin perceived the sound to grow gradually fainter, as, quitting the earthly building, it floated, heavenwards, away. While he pondered in his mind what these wondrous sounds might mean, he perceived the window of the oratory to open, and the bishop made a noise with his hand, as he was wont, and beckoned to him to come near, and, when he had obeyed the summons, he said, " Make haste to the Church, and cause the seven

"brethren to come hither, and do you come with them."
When the brethren were assembled, the bishop, knowing
that he was soon to leave them, gave them godly admoni-
tions that they should preserve the bond of peace among
themselves, and towards all men, and indefatigably practice
the rules of regular discipline, which they had been taught
by him, or had seen him observe, or had noticed in the
words or actions of former fathers. And, in the full per-
suasion that the day of his death was at hand, he added :
" that amiable guest, who was wont to visit our brethren,
" has vouchsafed, also, to come to me this day, and to call
" me out of this world. Return, therefore, to the Church,
" and speak to the brethren, that they, in their prayers,
" recommend my passage to the Lord, and that they be
" careful to provide for their own, the hour whereof is
" uncertain, by watching and prayer and good works."
" When he had spoken thus much and more," continues
Bede, " the good man gave them his blessing, and they
" went sorrowfully away."

No mortal ears had drunk in the angels' song, save those
of the bishop and his friend. When the brethren had
departed, Ovin returned alone, and prostrating himself on
the ground, said, " I beseech you father may I be permitted
to ask a question ?" "ask what you will" answered the
bishop, then he added, " I entreat you to tell me what song of
joy was that, which I heard coming upon this oratory, and

after some time returning to heaven? The bishop answered, " If you heard the singing, and know of the coming of the heavenly company, I command you, in the name of our Lord, that you do not tell the same to any before my death. They were angelic spirits, who came to call me to my heavenly reward, which I have always longed for, and they promised they would return seven days hence, and take me away with them."

The warning of his approaching death, thus marvellously given to him, we are told, was punctually fulfilled, for he was presently seized with a languishing distemper, attended with extreme debility, probably the yellow plague, which had already proved fatal to his brothers. This frightful scourge lasted many years, its fatality no doubt being vastly aggravated by the ignorance of sanatory laws, and the complete absence of anything like a knowledge of medicine.

Having partaken of the Holy Communion, and by prayer and meditation prepared for the inevitable change, Chad gradually sank beneath his malady, and on the 2nd March, 672, his earthly cares were ended, and his soul being delivered from the prison of the body, the angels, as had been promised, attended him, and carried him like another Lazarus to Abraham's bosom.

The bishop could hardly have been an old man when he died; but the chronology of his life is in many of its particulars obscure, and I have, therefore, reserved for a note some remarks upon the subject.

R

With the account of his death, we take our unwilling leave of his metrical biographer :— *

St. Chadde had only one year and a half scarcely
Been Bishop of Litchfield, ere he drew towards death.
One day he and brother Owyn, a monk, sate alone
In his cell, and the monks at Church were each one;
Then heard they the sweetest song that ever made a sound,
In heaven they thought that it began, and it came towards the ground.
All soft, downwards it came, until it came so nigh
That it alighted on the cell, upon the roof on high.
And half an hour it tarried right up upon the cell,
Of so merry melody may no tongue tell.
And afterwards, towards heaven, again the way it took,
With as merry a melody as it thither had come.
Well knew then, this holy man, how it should with him betide,
Afterwards all his monks to Church he sent anon.
He preached to them to be stedfast in our Lord's service,
And to love and keep their rule well and their order in all ways.
For that it was our Lord's will after him to send,
And from them, on the seventh day, to heaven he must wend.
For angels had brought him before such tiding
For to fetch him the seventh day, and to the joy of heaven bring.
Then after a short time this holy man in great sickness lay,
And died, as he had said, right on the seventh day.

* This poem, which is dated in the MS., 1370, has been attributed to Robert of Gloucester, who flourished about 1300.   I take the opportunity of mentioning the opinion of Professor Earle, kindly communicated to me, that this, though possible, is not likely to have been the case ; it being far more probable that the original composition belongs to the twelfth century.   It appears, adds Professor Earle, from the poem itself, that it was written whilst the Mercian See was at Chester, that is, before the year 1148, when it was restored to Lichfield by Bishop Roger.   See the Preface to this Volume.

With angels to heaven he went, as they brought him before tiding,
Now God, for the love of him, to such joy us bring.

Thus like the notes of a beautiful symphony passing gently away, closed the useful and honorable life of Chad, bishop of Lichfield, one of the most successful of the early preachers of the gospel in England, and one of the most popular of our national Saints.

Years rolled on. Chad had long been in the grave, though his virtues were still fresh in the memory of men, when it happened that one Hygbald, abbot of a monastery in Lincolnshire, possibly of that founded by Chad himself, crossed over into Ireland, to visit Egbert, whose acquantance Chad had made at Rathmelsigi.

The visit of the Lincolnshire abbot to Egbert, who must at this time have been advanced in years, recalled old memories; and the two ecclesiastics, after the manner of old men, fell to talking of their former friends, and of the holy fathers who had gone before them. Amongst others, mention was made of Chad, the late bishop of Lichfield, and of his happy departure from the world. Whereupon Egbert said, " I know a man in this island, still in the flesh, who when that prelate passed out of this world, saw the soul of his brother Cedd, with a company of angels descending from heaven, who, having taken his soul along with them, returned thither again." " Whether," says Bede, he said this of himself or some other, we do not certainly know, but the same being said by so great a man, there can be no doubt of the truth thereof."

Gladly would we believe, with the worthy historian, that his brother came to usher the dying saint to a joyful immortality. The records of such visions, frequently occur in the Lives of Saints. The death of Saint Hilda, for example, was miraculously made known to her friend Saint Ebba, by the sound of the passing bell, wafted across, from Whitby to Cumberland; and the vision of Saint Aidan departing to glory, strengthened Saint Cuthbert in the faith.

Whatever theory modern science might propound to account for the frequent recital of such visions, there can be no doubt of the good faith in which they were originally related by Bede and others, and may, even now, be regarded as a species of posthumous tribute to the piety and worth of those of whom such glorious things were told.

All the ancient chroniclers are agreed in commending the gentle virtues of Saint Chad, and we may well believe that there must have been something noble and beautiful in the characters of an epistle which was so " known and read of all men." He, indeed, added nothing to the literature of his age, or to the outward splendour of the Church he served so well; his doctrine and practice may not have perfectly agreed with those of more primitive times; nevertheless, his simple and earnest piety, the lofty view of his sacred

office, which he carried out in practice, and his truly apostolic
zeal, left a far deeper impress upon the minds of his countrymen, than the more specious qualities of Wilfrid, or the
towering ambition of Dunstan. The Anglican Communion
may justly count Saint Chad among the worthiest of her
ancient prelates; the Roman communion may, if she will,
claim him as one of her canonized saints; but, happily, he
belonged to that wider Communion of Saints whose only
head is the Founder of the Church Himself. His ground
of acceptance with God was the work of the great Atone-
ment, consummated in his soul; his claim upon our gratitude
rests upon the fervent and effectual zeal with which he
preached the Gospel of the Redeemer to our pagan forefathers.

The vividness of colouring, due to many stirring incidents,
has, doubtless, been wanting in the foregoing narrative of
Chad's life; but, just as the colours of the portrait of a saint,
in an old illuminated missal, have faded away, while the
golden halo remains untouched by age; so the holy zeal
and fervent piety of this ancient bishop remain above the
scorn of criticism, and beyond the reach of time; a burning
and shining light to all who are called to serve the same
Heavenly Master.

Later times have not reversed the verdict of his contemporaries, and we shall close this imperfect sketch of his life,
with some lines which were written of him, more than

a thousand years after his death, by a foreign ecclesiastic, and which though conceived in the spirit of mediæval superstition beautifully illustrate the Apostolic commendation that his praise was in all the Churches.

Mira hujus in Deum pietas fecit incertum
 utrum terræ cujus esset, an cœli :
  pastor populi fuit, divinis ipse deliciis pastus.
Cum sibi commissam accepit Merciorum gentem
  hoc sibi proposuit
 ut opulentas cœlo merces inferret :
 in vitæ cursu semper velificatus est tuto,
 nam si sonoræ circumtonarent procellæ
  lacrymis eas vincebat et gemitu :
 opponebat ardentia vota fulminibus
  suspiriis secundas evocabat auras.
Adfuerunt sæpe precanti cœlites
  musicum morituro concinnerunt melos
 pro nenia oden, pro epicedio epinicion,
  inter choreas et lyras efflavit animam
eosdem habuit symphoniacos moriens
   quos olim Deus oriens
 nisi forte significato quædam fuit
 non emortualem illum fuisse diem sed natalium.
Tunc maxime præsenti ope mortalibus adfuit
  cum ad immortales abiit,
 mira res ! currebant ad tumulum qui tumulari nolebant
  vitam suam propagabant illius cinere,
  devicta semper est mors
 quoties ejus tumuli decertavit in pulvere.

CHAPTER VIII.

Where'er one Levite in the temple keeps
  The watch-fires of his midnight prayer,
Or issuing thence, the eyes of mourners steeps
  In heavenly balm, fresh gathered there ;
Thus saints, that seem to die in earth's rude strife,
  Only win double life :
  They have but left our weary ways
To live in memory here, in Heaven by love and praise.
                                CHRISTIAN YEAR.

T H E life of a Canonized Saint would be incomplete, and lose much of its interest, without some account of the posthumous honours paid to his memory by the Roman Church.

No small portion of this superstitious and ignoble cultus fell to the share of Saint Chad, the particulars of which will exhibit a wide discrepancy between the simple missionary bishop, and the object of the future adoration of the multitude.

The earliest tribute of respect was paid to his earthly remains, which were, first of all, interred near the oratory where he had so devoutly prayed. Here he rested for twenty years, when Hedda, who succeeded Saxulf in the bishopric, erected a new church in honour of the Apostle Peter, into which the bones of his predecessor were carried, with all the reverence and respect shown in that age to the relics of saints.

In no long time, his ashes were thrown into the alembic of superstition, and pious respect grew into grovelling and abject worship, and the occasion of unblushing imposture. His bones, like those of other saints, were thought to be of miraculous efficacy in the cure of diseases; as though the crumbling dust were still redolent of the pure spirit once enshrined within it.   Crowds of persons, suffering from divers diseases, flocked to his tomb, as did the impotent folk of old to the porches of Bethesda, thinking, if they could but gather a handful of his hallowed dust and mingle it with water, they might be restored to health.   Nor were these benefits confined to human beings, but, even dumb animals drinking the same potent draught, were presently relieved from all their pains.   The very air of the place in which the saint rested from his labours, was a mighty anodyne to distracted souls; for one unhappy creature, who had been wandering about the neighbourhood, came, at nightfall, to his tomb, unregarded by the keepers of the place, and, having rested there all night, departed in the morning in his perfect senses, to the surprise and delight of all; "shewing, thus, plainly," says Bede, "that a cure had been performed on him, through the goodness of God."   But, as though these miracles were not sufficient for any man's remains to perform, the touch of Chad's bones is said, in the

Breviary, to have recalled departed souls from the gloomy shades of death :—

𝔄𝔟 𝔥𝔞𝔟𝔢𝔫𝔦𝔰 𝔪𝔬𝔯𝔱𝔦𝔰 𝔪𝔬𝔯𝔱𝔲𝔦 𝔢𝔵𝔠𝔦𝔱𝔞𝔫𝔱𝔲𝔯,
𝔉𝔲𝔯𝔦𝔬𝔰𝔦, 𝔟𝔦𝔫𝔠𝔲𝔩𝔦𝔰 𝔠𝔬𝔫𝔣𝔯𝔞𝔠𝔱𝔦𝔰, 𝔰𝔞𝔫𝔞𝔫𝔱𝔲𝔯.

The first receptacle of Chad's relics was in keeping with his own humble and unpretending character; being no more than a wooden monument, made like a little house covered in at the top, and having a hole in one side, through which the devout, who frequented the place, put in their hands and drew forth the health-giving dust.

In this humble shrine, what was supposed to be left of his bones, rested till the time of Bishop Roger, who, before his departure for the Holy Land, restored the episcopal see from Chester to Lichfield, and rebuilt the cathedral church in honour of the Virgin Mary and Saint Chad.

To this period is probably due the service in the Breviary for the *Translation of S. Chad.* The Translation of a Catholic Saint, from his earthly resting place, was no summary or irreverent proceeding, but was conducted with much pomp and ceremony. "Our forefathers," writes Dr. Lingard, "in their reverence for departed worth, went even further. Days were set apart, in the Calendar, to commemorate the auspicious days when their ashes were removed to a worthier resting place."

Every year, on the Sunday next before Ascension Day, was this tribute of superstitious respect paid to the relics of

Saint Chad. The prayer which was offered up on this occasion, exhibits a curious blending of superstition and piety :—

"O God, who grantest to us to celebrate the Translation "of the blessed Chad, thy Confessor and Bishop; we humbly "beseech Thee, that through his merits and prayers, we "may be translated from vice to virtue, and from our bonds "to the (heavenly) kingdom, through Jesus Christ our "Lord."

In the year 1296, Walter Langton, a prelate of munificent tastes, was raised to the see of Lichfield. Amongst other benefits conferred by him upon the cathedral and town, he laid the foundation of the exquisite Lady Chapel, whose lofty windows, and beautiful tracery, worthily adorn the noble pile of which they form a part. In this chapel the bishop placed, at the enormous cost of two thousand pounds, a beautiful shrine, to receive the relics of Saint Chad. Still further honour was done to the memory of the ancient saint by Bishop Galfrid Blythe, who, amongst other gifts to the cathedral, presented silver images of Saint Chad, and Saint Katharine.

When the dream of mediæval superstition was over, and the Iconoclasts of an iron age laid violent hands upon ecclesiastical wealth, these costly memorials would have shared the fate of other similar monuments, had not Bishop Lee pleaded hard with Henry VIII. that the chief ornament of his church might be saved from the grasp of the spoiler. The king had not forgotten the bishop who had secretly married him to Anne Boleyn, and in gratitude for his bride, the shrine of the saint was spared.

Though now become classic ground, as the birth-place of the author of *Rasselas*, and as possessing one of the choicest productions of our great sculptor's chisel, it is of the memories and traditions of its saintly bishop that Lichfield is chiefly and justly proud. The streets echo his name. The very brooks seem to murmur it. His gentle spirit would seem still to haunt the quiet precincts of the glorious minster, which, but for him, had never been. One of the most interesting features in the history of this, and many another Christian city, is its silent growth round the shrine of piety and religion, as the walls of ancient cities are fabled to have risen at the strains of the minstrel's lyre.

Though Chad had passed away ages before it was erected, Lichfield Cathedral is inseparably linked with his name and history. As the pilgrim treads, with reverent foot, the floor of the presbytery, his eyes are arrested by the medallions of incised marble, in which have been traced some of the well-known incidents in the saint's life.* Passing outside, he will see among the "carven saints," which adorn the west front, his statue occupying the place of honour.

* See illustrations, opposite to pages 36 and 40, from the designs of the Rev. E. R. Pitman, of Rugeley.

Poetry has not been behind sculpture in paying him her tribute of respect.   Drayton, with one stroke of his pen, does honour to Lichfield and its ancient bishop :—

> Lichfield hath those no whit less famous nor less good,
> The first of whom is that most reverent Chad,
> In those religious times for holinesse that had
> The name above the best that lived in those days,
> That stories have been stuft with his abundant praise,
> Who on the see of York being formerly instaul'd,
> Yet when back to that place Saint Wilfrid was recal'd,
> The seat to that good man he willingly resign'd,
> And to the quiet close of Lichfield him confin'd.

As the patron saint of Lichfield, Chad was long supposed to have the city under his especial protection.   During the Parliamentary wars, Lord Brooke laid siege to the place, which was held on behalf of the king, on which occasion the beautiful cathedral suffered severely.   It was, however, gratefully noted by the royalists that the republican leader was killed by a shot fired from Saint Chad's cathedral, on Saint Chad's day, to which circumstance the author of *Marmion* refers in the well-known lines :—

> Fitz-Eustace' care
> A pierced and mangled body bare
> To moated Lichfield's lofty pile ;
> And there, beneath the southern aisle,
> A tomb, with Gothic sculpture fair,
> Did long Lord Marmion's image bear,
> Now vainly for its site you look ;
> 'Twas levelled when fanatic Brook
> The fair cathedral storm'd and took;
> But, thanks to heaven and good Saint Chad !
> A guerdon meet the spoiler had.

This curious incident is referred to, in a still more striking manner, by Dr. South, in a sermon on the words, " God loveth the gates of Zion more than all the dwellings of Jacob." " Nor," says that learned divine, " is that instance to be passed over of a commander in the parliamentary army, who, coming to rifle and deface the Cathedral at Lichfield, solemnly, at the head of his troops, begged of God to shew some remarkable token of his approbation or dislike of the work they were going about. Immediately after which, he was shot in the forehead by a deaf and dumb man ; and this was on Saint Chad's day, the name of which Saint that Church bore, being dedicated to God in memory of the same : where we see that, as he asked of God a sign, so God gave him one in the forehead, and that with such a mark as he is like to be known by all posterity."*

On the east side of the city is the church of Saint Chad, de Stowe, to the north-west of which was the famous oratory of the bishop, already referred to. " It was the custom, in former times," observes Dr. Stukeley, " to erect churches to the east of the cells of recluses famous for sanctity." The same author mentions that Chad's oratory was only pulled down a few years before the year in which he wrote (1736); but this could hardly have been the actual scene of the saint's devotions, and of the wonderful vision described in the preceding chapter.

* Sermons, vol. I,, p. 185. Dugdale alludes to this, also, in his "View of the late troubles in England," p. 117.

Close to the cell, was the celebrated well* or fountain which takes its name from the Saint. At the bottom of this cell there is a stone upon which Chad is said to have been in the habit of standing naked to pray. This singular method of performing his devotions, may have been derived from the Irish monks who often carried their austerities to an absurd extent, but far more probably, the well was used as a baptistery for the immersion of converts. It should, however, be said that the quainter notion has the partial support of the Breviary :—

> Qui sic fontem frigidum orans introivit,
> Et non corpus calido balneo nutrivit.

†Dr. Plot in his Natural History of Staffordshire, takes notice of this well, and refers to the superstitious practice of the people of adorning the wells on Holy Thursday, with flowers and the boughs of trees, and reading thereat the gospel for the day. This practice, obviously of pagan origin, had never been publicly sanctioned and was condemned in several provincial councils.

An entertaining account is given in Hone's Year Book, of a well existing until quite modern times, in London, and called Chad's Well, the water of which was sold to valetudinarians at sixpence a glass. For this, or some other reason, Chad has the credit of being the patron saint of

---

* Dr. Stukeley made drawings of both Oratory and Fountain.
† Quoted in Harwood's Antiquities of Lichfield.

medicinal springs, but I have not discovered any other ground for the notion than popular tradition.

A glance at the *Constitutions* published by successive bishops of Lichfield, will show the estimation in which their illustrious predecessor was held in Roman Catholic times. The treasurer of the Chapter was required to furnish two wax tapers and to keep one lamp perpetually burning before his altar. Bishop Hugo Nonant, assigned, as one of the perquisites of the Sacristan, all the wax tapers offered in the chapel of Saint Chad at Stow, excepting those placed at the feet of the saint's image. At Chadshunt, in the same county, there was a small oratory containing an image of Saint Chad, and a well bearing his name; the former of which was served by a priest, who received as much as £16 a year from the pilgrims who resorted thither. In connection with these vested interests created by Saint Chad, may be mentioned, an annual payment called *Chad's Pennies** or *Farthings*, formerly included among the Easter Dues, for the purpose of hallowing the Font for Christenings.

A blithe day in Lichfield, in those times, was the 2nd of March. On that day the cathedral was gaily festooned with silken banners, and hangings. Many a taper lighted up the altar of the saint, and the notes of the full choral service chanted by the cathedral clergy, resounded through 'the long drawn aisles' and beneath the 'fretted roof' of the noble minster.

* Baptism was, in former times, administered only on the Eves of Easter and Pentecost.

Welcome, especially, must the advent of this day have been to the resident Canons, for it was ordained, by Bishop Newland, that, whereas, on ordinary days, they were to receive one shilling for their stipend, and, on double festivals, a like increase in their pay, on this auspicious festival, and three others, they were to have ten shillings, for their guerdon.

The service drawn up for S. Chad's day, occurs in most of the "*Uses*" or versions of the Breviary. The least objectionable form of the service is contained in the Aberdeen Breviary* consisting of nine lections taken from Bede, with an anthem, and a collect addressed to God, in which the merits of Chad are pleaded, but the saint is not himself invoked :—

"O God, who hast adorned the Universal Church with "the merits of thy Saints, grant, we beseech Thee, that all "who implore the aid of the blessed Chad, may receive an "effectual answer to their healthful supplication."

A similar service was observed in the diocese of York, where the people naturally held the memory of their first native bishop in just respect. In this and other Breviaries, curiously enough, Lastingham, or Lastingay, is said to be in the island of Lindisfarne.

A more developed service than either of the preceding is found in the once celebrated "*Use*" of Sarum. It

---

* A beautiful fac-simile edition of this Breviary has been printed by the Bannatyne Club.

consists of three lections either founded on, or taken from the Latin text of Bede, with psalms, responsories and anthems. The Sarum Breviary was that most extensively used in the Church of England, but a special rubric allowed the Church of Lichfield, to have fuller services of its own in honour of its patron saint, which I proceed to describe.

In virtue of the privileges retained by local churches when they accepted the Sarum Breviary, Saint Chad's day was celebrated at Lichfield with great pomp and solemnity, as one of the principal festivals of the church. Amid the fragrance of incense, and the solemn music of the cathedral choir, the people were called upon to celebrate the memory of their ancient saint. The service commenced at the Vespers of the vigil, or eve before, with the following anthem :—

> Germanorum quatuor unus est beatus
> Cedda, quorum quilibet erat consecratus

Other anthems and psalms followed, with capitulum responsory, &c. In one of the antiphons which may thus be freely rendered, the Saint, as though he could hear the prayers of the people, is directly invoked :—*

"O Holy Chad, be thou our advocate with the Lord, "that He may rule and guide us to heavenly mansions, "where with thee, and with the saints, we may for ever "dwell."

* For a summary of the controversy respecting the Invocation of Saints, see Palmer's Antiquities of the British Ritual. Vol. I. 289—292.

T

At an early hour on the following morning commenced the solemnities proper to the Saint's day. This was at the service called in later times *Matutini,* but formerly known as *Nocturns,* from the ancient Christians having observed it at night. It was divided into three parts, corresponding to the three canonical hours of which Nocturns formerly consisted, but forming apparently one continuous service. To each of these parts were assigned, on the day in question, three of the nine short lections appropriated to the service and for the most part taken from Bede. Several of the antiphons and responsories from this service have already been given. The following lines present a strange if not beautiful application of Scripture :—

> ℞. Postquam Cedde lux presens clauditur,
> Laus ipsius a plebe canitur,
> Hostes vincens hic non devincitur.
>
> ℟. Ais unguenti dum pixis frangitur,
> Cunctis patet nec plus absconditur.

In this portion of the service, the Scriptures were not altogether neglected. Besides several Psalms, the Parable of the Talents, from the Gospel of S. Matthew, was not inappropriately introduced, while respect was paid to the writings of the Fathers in the recitation of a homily of Pope Gregory.

Following upon the Matutini, or Nocturns, was the service held at a later hour called *Lauds* corresponding to the ancient matins. One of the antiphons at this service is to the following effect :—

"O pious bishop, Saint Chad, pray the Lord for us, that "we,- who have provoked Him by our sins, may not be "delivered to torments, but may enjoy perpetual bliss in "heaven."

The return of Vespers completed this long service, and the Festival of Saint Chad ended with the words of solemn, though unenlightened, prayer.

Reference has been made to the service for the Translation of Saint Chad. The longer form comprised, besides the anthems and collect, a portion of the fifteenth chapter of S. John, an extract from a homily of Saint Augustine, upon the same scripture, and two lections from Bede describing the translation of his relics and the miracles performed at his tomb. For the private use of persons who might have a special devotion to the saint on account of some benefit supposed to have been derived through his intercession, the service last mentioned could be shortened, in which case, the portion belonging to the first Vespers was used.

The *Constitutions* of Bishop Hugo ordered that a *missa de jejunio* should be celebrated in the chapter-house on the festival of S. Chad; in connection with which it may be mentioned that there is in the Sarum Missal, printed by Bembolt, at Paris, in 1513, a service commemorative of S. Chad, composed of prayers in his especial honour, and of prayers, &c., suited to the commemoration of any Bishop and Confessor. The prayers composed for this service do not differ in spirit from those contained in the Breviary, and it will not therefore be needful to set them forth in full; the whole of the services, however, drawn up in honour of S. Chad, fairly illustrate the spirit in which these devotions were conceived and expressed, and which amply justified their banishment from the Reformed Service Books.

The date of Saint Chad's canonization and of his first appearance in the Calendar and Breviary I have not been able to discover, though further research might possibly clear up the point. Prior to the tenth century, persons eminent for sanctity had been venerated as saints in various local churches, and the mention of *Chad's day* in the Martyrology, erroneously attributed to Bede, seems to imply that, at a very early period, a day had been set apart in honour of the Saint. The service for his day seems to rest upon the authority of a Provincial Council,* of the date and place of which I find, however, no record.

Though Chad had no claim to the aureole, his name is inscribed in various martyrologies, and in the Breviaries he is invoked as a Bishop and Confessor. In Whitford's Martyrology printed in London in 1526, he is commemorated as "a bysshop and a confessour of synguler vertue, and many myracles;" in the Martyrologies of Wion and

* MS., Ee-2-2, Cambridge University Library.

Wilson, his name is inscribed ; and in the well-known work of John Capgrave, his life is set forth at length from the narrative of Bede.

Besides the notices which occur of Saint Chad in the volumes of Baronius, Trithemius, Harpsfeld, Mabillon, the *Acta Sanctorum* of the Bollandists, and a multitude of ecclesiastical histories, his name is held up to the veneration of the faithful in the Cologne Martyrology, printed in the year 1490, and also in the Roman Martyrology, which quotes the history of Bede as its authority. Even the Lutheran Centuriators* of Madgeburg, did not count our humble English bishop beneath their notice, and seem to express their belief in the miracles, attributed to his relics by Bede.

In the "Calendar of the Prayer Book," the name of Saint Chad is still retained on the 2nd March, for what reason it is not easy to determine.† In the old Roman Calendar he is a Red-letter Saint, but was shorn of that dignity by the Reformers. In connection with the stormy season of the year, in which Chad was wont to be honoured, may be mentioned a local rhyme, of a not very flattering character, still heard in the county of Norfolk :—

> First comes David,
> Then comes Chad,
> Then comes Win'ald roaring mad.

* Quoted in Cressy's Church History. † The names of some saints were retained in the Reformed Calendar for purely secular reasons. See Wheatley, Blakeney, and others.

This Saint is usually represented in ecclesiastical art, as in the frontispiece to this volume, with a branch as his emblem, the significance of which is, however, uncertain. It may perhaps be a token of his fruitful labours as a missionary, or possibly an allusion to the branches with which he is said in the legend, to have covered the hart he had tamed; on the whole, however, I am disposed to derive the significance of the emblem from the gospel read for the Translation of Saint Chad, implying that he was a fruitful branch of the Living Vine. This emblem may be seen delineated in a very simple form upon the Clog Almanacs, or Runic Calendars, specimens of which are preserved in the British Museum, and other places. The existence of this memorial of the Saint upon these simple contrivances, contributed largely to his popularity, and long made his name a "household word" in England.

It is mentioned in that most interesting little work, " *The Calendar of the Prayer Book, illustrated,*" that in a Roman Catholic Church, named in his honour, recently erected "by " Mr. Pugin at Birmingham, he is represented carrying a " Church in his hand, as the founder of the Mother Church " of the diocese."

In Roman Catholic times, images were frequently made of Saint Chad, which became objects of superstitious reverence. Mention has been made of that at Chadshunt, and of the silver image in Lichfield Cathedral. From the authority last quoted we learn that at the fall of the old Church of Saint Chad, in Shrewsbury, in the year 1788, among the few things which escaped destruction, was an ancient wooden figure of the bishop, which is still preserved in the new Church. The carver has represented him in his pontifical robes and mitre, with a Latin Bible in his right hand, and the crozier or pastoral staff in his left. Gough in his "History of Croyland" mentions that over the door entering from the belfry into that Church, were two wooden statues of Saint David, and Saint Chad, which Dr. Stukeley had conveyed to Stamford, where they continued till they were finally taken to adorn the garden of a member of the Doctor's family at Holbeach. So much for the glory of a Saint!

But though Saint Chad is no longer an object of ignorant superstition, his name is not likely to be forgotten, in this country at least. Thirty one churches, dedicated in his name, chiefly within the limits of his ancient diocese, attest the popularity he nobly won and still enjoys.

The revival of religion and learning, during the Reformation of the Church, justly taught men to reserve their prayers for that Great Being to whom alone they are due. The greater part of the honours paid to our saint, described in the preceding pages, have but little warrant from sound reason, or true piety. But, carrying our thoughts back to the days when pagan darkness brooded over the infant

Commonwealth of England, it is impossible not to feel interested in the four brothers, who carried the torch of the Gospel through the length and breadth of our land, but whose labours are still but dimly remembered. Our prayers, indeed, we must withhold, but we need not grudge to their memories our grateful recollections.

No authentic written remains of Saint Chad have survived, but, in the Cathedral Library of Lichfield, an ancient manuscript is preserved, which is known by the name of "Chad's Gospel." It was presented to the Library by Frances, Duchess of Somerset, and was formerly preserved in a case beneath a portrait of the illustrious donor, the doors of which receptacle bore the following inscription :—

Sanctiss. Liber
qui intus reconditur
sicut in arca est collocatus
Thesaurus fuit olim et deliciæ
Illustrissimæ Dominæ
Domicæ Franciscæ Devereux
Ducissæ Somersetensis
Cujus pulcherrimam Imaginem
Auspice Lector
et Venerare.

Hoc Immerito.
Clarissimi enim heroici
"Gemmam hanc cui aurum est vile"
Unà cum prope mille aliis Volumen
Dilectæ suæ et semper memo :
Ecclesiæ Cathedral : de Lichfield
Majorem Dei Gloriam et
bonarum Literarum ubertatem
D.   D.   F.   *

Pater noster qui es incoe
lus sanctetur nomen tuum
Adueniat regnum tuum fiat
uoluntas tua sicut incoelo
& interra panem nostrum
super sub statiadem danc
bis odie &demitte . nobis
debita nostra sicut &nos
dimissimus debitoribus nos
tris &ne nos inducas
intemptationem sed libera
nos ꝺinxle ꝉꝰ

The Lords Prayer from a Manuscript of the 7th Century, (St Chad's Gospel)
in the Library, Lichfield Cathedral.

This precious relic of antiquity has been transferred to the case in which the other manuscripts are kept. It is believed to have been preserved during the Civil War, and the wanton destruction, by the Puritans, of Lichfield Cathedral, and all its ornaments, by the Rev. William Higgins, Precentor of the Cathedral, called by Dugdale, "chief chante of Lichfield." The volume, which contains 236 pages, has recently been rebound.

A minute description of this famous Codex would not come within the scope of the present work, but a few particulars respecting it, derived from various sources, may not be unacceptable, while the printed illustrations* may afford some idea of ancient drawing and calligraphy.

The text, which is in Latin, is written throughout in the Anglo-Saxon character, and contains the Gospels of S. Matthew, S. Mark, and a portion of S. Luke. The initial letter of each Gospel is intricately formed and beautifully illuminated, and occupies the entire length of the page on which it stands. The Gospels of SS. Mark and Luke are preceded by rude portraits of those Evangelists. The former is represented as holding a book, with both hands upon his breast ; the head is surrounded by a plain yellow nimbus with a white border, over which is extended the symbolical lion, but without the wings which usually accompany it, and holding a book in its four paws. S. Luke, who

* I am indebted to the kindness of W. C. Gresley, Esq., for permission to use these illustrations.

appears to be standing in a kind of rostrum, is drawn with long flowing hair, and having his head surrounded by a purple nimbus, decorated with three crosses ; the whole figure being surmounted by a winged calf, the emblem of that Evangelist in sacred art. One leaf of the Codex has rude delineations of the Evangelic symbols, and on the reverse side, an elaborate cruciform design, said to be equal in minuteness and accuracy of detail, and in richness of colouring, to the most perfect designs in the Gospel of Lindisfarne.

The origin of the Codex is very uncertain, but various marginal entries, indicating the use of the volume in judicial proceedings, seem to trace it to the diocese of Llandaff. All scholars, who have examined this evangelistarium, ascribe to it a high antiquity, while the writer from whom the above description is chiefly taken, thinks it quite possible that it may have been written by Saint Chad himself, and hence its designation. *It is said, however, to be the production of a very indifferent Latin scholar, on which account, in spite of its quaint devices, I am content to leave its authorship in obscurity.

Though the services in the Breviaries, in their honour, were not likely to have been generally understood, and were, therefore, the less mischievous, the merits of the saints were not suffered to be forgotten, for want of being commemorated

* Nares MS. Cat. quoted in Botfield's Notes on the Cathedral Libraries.

Aug.^{tn} C. Gresley 1860

*Emblems of the 4 Evangelists from a M.S. of the 7th Century. (St Chad's Gospel.)
in the Library, Lichfield Cathedral.*

in the vernacular. Besides the metrical versions of his life, in the old English tongue, which have come down to us, there is preserved, among the Bodleian MSS., an Anglo-Saxon Homily, drawn up for use on Saint Chad's day, in which his virtues are duly set forth, from Bede, for the admiration of the multitude.*

The history of this interesting relic of antiquity is, I believe, not known; but it is, no doubt, of very ancient origin. A tone of chaste and archaic simplicity pervades this ancient tribute to departed worth. It adds nothing, indeed, to our knowledge of his life, but that life seems to be invested with a deeper and more abiding interest, when narrated in the homely, but expressive, language in which Chad clothed the message of the Gospel to his Mercian flock. The beginning of it, which has been translated as follows, may serve as a specimen of the form in which these compositions were drawn up; "Dearly beloved men and "brethren, I will now begin to tell you the life of that "holy man, St. Chad, the bishop : how he did in the "Bishopdom, and ere he came to the Bishopdom ; though "we may not, by any means, reach to all the mighty "wonders of his work : for that it was strongly in him

---

* Professor Earle, who has kindly examined this document for me, from a transcript furnished by Mr. G. Parker, of Oxford, observes that "the Saxon is very interesting, "being not the ordinary Anglo-Saxon, but in the Middle-Anglian dialect, a dialect "that stretched from Lichfield to Peterborough. Indeed it may well have been made "(the translation from Bede) at Lichfield itself. The comparison of it with the Anglo-"Saxon version, which is commonly called Alfred's Version, is extremely interesting."

" not to seek praise from men ; so strongly, that with all his
" might and main he would shun the notice of men."

And with the conclusion of the homily, we may fitly, but
unwillingly, take our leave of the saintly bishop :—

" Pray we now to the undivided Trinity, that we may be
" helped with the prayers of this most holy man, St. Chad,
" and that we may earn for ourselves to come to the fellow-
" ship of holy bishops and blessed spirits, through the
" forgiveness of our Lord and Saviour Jesus Christ, who
" liveth and reigneth with the Father, and with the Holy
" Ghost, world without end."

NOTES.

A.

I HAVE adhered, throughout the text, to the popular spelling of Chad's name, but it is right to apprise the reader that in ancient authors it varies considerably. The most frequent form in the chroniclers is Ceadda, this, however, is sometimes shortened into Cedda, as in the Breviaries. In early English, the variations Chade and Chadde occur, while the still shorter forms of Cead and Ced are occasionally met with, before the spelling settled down into Chadd, and, lastly, Chad. The most curious variation, however, is exhibited in the cloister legend, where, not without an apparent tinge of irreverent familiarity, we make the acquaintance of Chaddy !

B.

Two popular explanations of the meaning of Lastingham have been referred to in the foregoing pages, but scholars seem to be agreed that the true etymology of Lestingaen is the Water of the Lestings, that is, of the family bearing that name, and Lestingham, their home. The name is spelt in a great variety of ways, nor is it an easy matter to track the original form through this labyrinth of changes. Bede spells the name Laestingaen. In the Saxon Homily for Saint Chad's day, written in the Mid-Anglian dialect, the spelling is Læstinga æg. In the Doomsday Record it became Lestingeham; while Florence of Worcester gives another variation in Lestingaig, Symeon of Durham in Lestingahen, Gervase of Canterbury in Lastingei, and Stubbs in the ACTA PON. EBOR. in Lastyngaen. In the old Parish Registers we find Lastinga. In an ancient will, printed by the Surtees Society, the testator, Ion of Croxton, bequeathes 'to Alise, of Lastyngham, ij. з. and russet cloth to make her a cloke with.' Last of all, I must not omit to notice the spelling which received the sanction of the Church, viz., Lastingay.

C.

Throughout this volume I have taken for granted, in common with most writers who have mentioned the place, that Lastingham is the Lestingaen of Bede. The identity, however, has been disputed. In a paper, read before the Yorkshire Archæological Society, Mr. Haigh, of Birmingham, seeks to prove that the well-known village of Kirkdale is the site of the monastery founded by Cedd, and that our Lastingham was a dependent cell belonging to that house. With much diffidence, I venture to call in question the principal arguments by which this conclusion is supported.

It is argued, in the first place, that the change of original form of the name, Lestingaen, into Lestingham, was in the last degree unlikely to have taken place after the estate became church land. But the fact that the change, if ever it took place, remained in force with respect to what is admitted to have been church land, deprives this argument of any weight. I believe, however, it would be difficult to disprove that Lestingaen and Lestingham were forms of the name used at the same period.

An argument of a more historical character is based upon an inscription found on a cross built into one of the walls of Kirkdale Church. Mr. Haigh thus deciphers it :—

> To the memory of Oidilvald, Cedd placed this stone.

Now the king, mentioned in this inscription, in granting an estate to Cedd for the foundation of a monastery, had in view a place of sepulture for himself and family. Hence, it is argued that the inscription indicates his burial place, and, therefore, the position of Bede's Lastingaen. But the interpretation of the inscription, and the history of the cross on which it is found, are obviously too precarious to serve as the foundation of a solid argument. Accordingly, another inscription, over the western door, is appealed to. It is to the effect that one, Orm, the son of Gamal, bought Saint Gregory's minster when it was in ruins, and rebuilt it in honour of Gregory. This, unquestionably, favours the supposition that there had been a monastery in this place, but it proves too much, for we know, from Bede, that the monastery of Lastingham was dedicated to Saint Mary, not to mention that a Celtic monk was not very likely to have built a monastery in honour of Pope Gregory.

But the claim of Lastingham does not rest upon negative arguments. Stephen of Whitby, who wrote an account of the foundation of S. Mary's, York, took refuge, he informs us, in the monastery of Lastingham, FORMERLY celebrated for the number and piety of its monks. Stephen goes on to say that he caused to be built all that was needful for the accommodation of his monks ; a proceeding harmonizing well with the Lastingham ruined by the Danes, but in no way answering to the condition of Kirkdale, which, in Stephen's time, must have been all but fresh from the mason's chisel. Moreover, there is an unbroken chain of documentary evidence connecting the present Lastingham with the Lastingham of Stephen of Whitby, and the Doomsday Record, in both of which authorities we find Appleton, Spaunton, and Hutton, mentioned in connection with that place of which they have long constituted townships. Considering, then, that (1) there is no evidence, whatever, of the change in name from Lastingham to Kirkdale ; (2) that the antiquity of Lastingham is beyond question, and its extent as a monastic establishment proved from the traces of foundations, which, from time to time, have been laid bare, and (3) the mention of Lastingham, with its townships, in the public records ; I conclude, that if a monastery was subsequently erected at Kirkdale, Lastingham cannot, thereby, be divested of its hallowed associations as the tranquil retreat of Chad and his pious companions.

D.

As Lastingham occupies so important a position in the preceeding pages, a short account of its celebrated crypt may not be unacceptable. There is no record of its erection, and, consequently, antiquarians are divided in their opinions as to the date of its architecture. The Rev. W. Eastmead gives the following description :—"From the window, through which the light gleams, giving a view of the whole extent of it, (the east end of the church being on the brow of a steep hill) the scene is interesting to astonishment. Here you perceive the massy arches, ranged in perspective ; you behold the huge cylindrical pillars, and their variously sculptured capitals—each one differing from the other, all in the real Saxon style ; to this, add the groined roof, and the stairs at the west end, leading up to the church, enveloped in a luminous obscurity from the scanty light admitted by the window in the east. From the account, given by Bede, that the body of Cedd was buried on the right side of the altar, one may suppose that this crypt was made after the erection of the church, though the time cannot be ascertained."

In a less florid manner, the late Rev. R. Harrison writes of the church and crypt as follows :—"In itself it is only partially of Saxon character ; but its crypt, which is pure Saxon, is, perhaps, the best specimen in existence of that order of architecture, and commands the attention of every antiquary who visits it."

In Raine's ANTIQUITIES OF DURHAM, a very high antiquity is claimed for the crypt of Lastingham. "I have before me," says that learned writer, "two very interesting prints of the church of Lastingham, in its present state, by Halfpenny of York. The external view carries with it the undoubted proof of high antiquity. The absciss, or semicircular termination, is copied from the heathen basilicæ, which were in many instances converted into places of Christian worship, and the internal view of the crypt exhibits manifest proofs of the most early antiquity. The large square pedestal, the short circular column, the rudely sculptured cap, and the absence of ribbed groining, induce me to believe that the church of Lastingham, if not the original building of Cedd, is, at least, the most ancient ecclesiastical structure in the kingdom."

On the other hand, Mr. Britton considers it to be a specimen of the early Norman style, and to form part of the monastery erected during the rule of Abbot Stephen, since it corresponds with the other known crypts of the Norman age, in the massive character, forms and ornaments of the columns, and the simplicity of the groining and arches.

With reference to this latter view, it may be observed that Stephen, though he mentions having erected all things needful for the monks, says nothing of so important a building as the Crypt; while the short time in which his enemies left him in peace, renders it improbable that he could have executed so extensive a work, unless, like the Jews, the monks worked with the sword in one hand and a trowel in the other. On the other hand, Bede expressly mentions a stone church as having been built here, to which period, in the absence of a unanimous professional verdict, it may be allowable to refer the crypt.

Some interesting Roman and Celtic relics are preserved in the crypt; amongst others, the quaint looking figures represented on pages 19 and 57. Tradition speaks of an underground passage, connecting the crypt of Lastingham with the nunnery of Rosedale; if such there were, one might truly say

facilis descensus Averno ;

*   *   *   *   *

Sed revocare gradum superasque evadere ad auras
Hoc opus, hic labor est.

E.

The chronology of Chad's life, and his age at death, can only be approximately determined from the few notes of time furnished by Bede. We learn from that historian, (1), that he studied with Egbert, afterwards Abbat of Iona, when they were YOUTHS TOGETHER in Ireland, and that the latter was born in 639. But as Chad died in 672, he would have been but 33, if no older than Egbert. We must, therefore, suppose the two to have studied together, but without being, strictly speaking, contemporaries. We learn (2), that Chad was a disciple of Saint Aidan, and, in all probability, one of the twelve whom he gathered around him on his arrival at Lindisfarne in 635. Assuming him to have been about fifteen at this time, we should have 620 as the date of his birth, and fifty-two for his age at death by pestilence, in 672.